Novels by David Czaplicki

The Mars Trilogy
Mars 185

The Man in the Woods

The Superstitions
Hidden Secrets

The Superstitions
Hidden Secrets

by

David Czaplicki

2023 : White Solar Press

ISBN: 978-1-7377824-2-1

To Sandy

For her unwavering support

1

A series of volcanic eruptions between 20.5 and 18 million years occurred in what is the present-day southwest. The formation of volcanoes and volcanic domes followed by the caldera, a crater formed by a collapse of the mouth of the volcanoes. This particular caldera filled up with volcanic ash and lava flows composed of dacite lava and rhyolitic tuff. A mountain was formed as the eruptions ended, and the filled caldera pushed upwards. The Superstition Mountains were formed.

* * *

Between 1250 and 1450, several thousand people of different cultures settled in these mountains. They became known as Salado. Hunting and farming were their primary activities. They roamed these mountains and drew on the walls pictures of the longhorn sheep they hunted, pictures of their clan, and pictures of their gods.

In 1540, the Spanish Conquistador Francisco Vázquez de Coronado set out to find the mystical "Seven Cities of Gold". Scout teams explored the Superstition Mountains. The native Indians refused to help them as it was sacred ground and those who trespassed would face horrible deaths. Many conquistadors began to vanish, only to be found later decapitated and mutilated. The conquistadors finally fled, never to return.

Some of the early American settlers called them the "Killer Mountains". Some Apache believed that a hole leading down to the lower world, the place white men call hell, is located in the Superstition Mountains.

* * *

Cal Ligai had just graduated from training as a patrol deputy for Pinal County in Arizona. During his first week, he was temporarily assigned to the headquarters in Florence, Arizona until his official assignment was given to him.

He sat at his desk daydreaming about being out on patrol when he overheard a call over the radio, another missing hiker in the Superstitions. It was a hot June afternoon and a person without water might not last too long in those mountains. Cal overheard the dispatcher asking for a few more deputies to help. Cal's eyes met the dispatchers. He couldn't read his lips as he talked to one of the senior deputies.

"Ligai, are you ready to take a drive with me?" came the deep voice from the senior deputy.

"Absolutely," Cal replied as he gathered his belongings.

"You ready to sweat your ass off? There is a missing hiker in the "Supes", crazy fool, this time of year in this heat no one should go out alone, they may never make it out," the senior deputy said as they made their way to the pickup.

Cal had only seen the deputy, Deputy Anderson, a few times at headquarters, but he had heard of his reputation. Old school, tough, and didn't care about anyone's feelings.

"I hiked in the Superstitions many times as a kid," Cal replied with no response from Anderson. "Of course, it was in winter," Cal hesitantly added.

"I never enjoy hiking. Never saw the sense of it," Anderson replied.

The two deputies turned up on Highway 60 at Florence Junction. Still, twenty miles away, the Superstitions stood solitary and enigmatic, emanating an air of mysticism. The cacti were becoming more numerous, filling the landscape. They made their way through Gold Canyon, which was once a small bedroom community and was now growing every year. The sheriff's truck turned up Mountain View, which ran parallel to the front of the Superstition Mountains. The two-lane highway was scattered with small ranches and Adobe homes. Saguaros filled the landscape, creating a cactus forest.

"They've set up a command post in Lost Dutchman State Park. From there they'll tell us where we can help," Anderson said as they turned north onto Route 88, the Apache Trail.

Cal looked up at the Superstitions and could see two helicopters above the mountains.

"Yep, the Lost Dutchman. Grew up hearing about those stories," Cal answered.

"Wild bullshit. Half of these people we rescue in these mountains have dreams of finding his gold. They all believe the tales of the Lost Dutchman," Anderson scoffed his reply as they entered the state park.

As they were directed by the state park employee, Cal noticed various vehicles from other law enforcement agencies, including Search and Rescue and rangers from the Tonto National Forest.

Cal and Anderson got out of the vehicle and headed to a group reviewing a map on the hood of one of the pickup trucks. The deputy pointing to the map looked up at the two and acknowledged them.

"Thanks for helping. We're running out of daylight. It's going to get a lot tougher when that sun sets."

"We're happy to help," Cal replied as he looked around at the group. A few deputies from the Maricopa County sheriff's department, both Cal's age, held out their hand to Cal and Anderson.

"Thanks for getting here so quickly."

Cal also noticed many volunteers and a younger Native American woman who was a Tonto National

Forest Ranger. Cal was surprised to see someone from the Tonto National Forest Ranger involved in the hike, as they rarely help search for a lost hiker.

"As I was saying," the team leader said as he pointed to the map, "We have a helicopter covering this area. We've got over a dozen people headed up various trails. If the rest of us split up, maybe take different forks on the trails, maybe we'll get lucky." He looked at the two sheriffs from Maricopa County. "If you two could head up to the First Water trailhead and go due north onto the Hackberry trail. It's a bit far, but maybe he's there."

The two deputies shook their heads in acknowledgment. The team leader turned to Cal and Anderson. "If you two also go down the road to the First Water trailhead and go up the Dutchman's trail. Again, we have a white male, 26 years of age, thin, 5'10", brown hair, and believed to be wearing a yellow shirt."

"Not a problem," Cal replied, looking at the group.

Anderson was looking down at the map. "You realize we'll be leaving Pinal County," he snickered.

The young Tonto National Forest Ranger looked up at Anderson. "Once you're a half mile up the trail, you'll be back in Pinal."

The team leader glanced at Anderson and then gave different locations to the other remaining people.

"Ladies and gentlemen let's keep our eyes open. We'll be running out of daylight before you know it," the team leader said as he folded the map.

Cal and Anderson got into the pickup and headed up County 88 and turned down a dirt road. The sign leading down the road just said, "First Water Trailhead". They drove down the primitive road until they got to a parking area at the end with a marker for Dutchman's Trail.

Cal grabbed a backpack and added additional bottles of water to it. He looked at Anderson slowly getting out.

"You ready, boy?" Anderson asked.

"Sure am," he replied as he watched Anderson make his way to the trailhead entrance. "I wonder if we should split up. Maybe I go at a faster pace and get more distance. You slowly scan the trail on each side."

Anderson wiped the sweat off his forehead. "You know, that's not a bad idea. You're younger and faster, probably make some ground quickly. Like you said, I'll scan the area that you run through."

Cal not only thought it was a better idea, but he thought Anderson would slow him down.

"Ligai let's keep in contact over the radio, but no need to let everyone know our plan," Anderson said as Cal separated from him as he picked up the pace.

"I totally agree. You have enough water?" he asked Anderson.

"I'm good."

Cal found a quick pace where he didn't get winded yet covered a lot of ground. The brush was still thick and green as the hundred-plus temperatures were not yet constant. Cal stopped a few times to grab a drink and call out the young man's name.

Over the radio, he heard some of the team check in with locations. He even heard Anderson check in with a location and after Cal thought about it, Anderson's guess on Cal's location was spot on.

As Cal had stopped again for water, he could see the bright sun in the west slowly settle into the sky. It wouldn't be long before the Dutchman Trail was in the shadow of the mountains.

Cal crossed over the same creek bed many times, sometimes there was a slow running trickle, other times small, stagnant pools of water. His radio crackled with static as he stopped to listen to the conversation.

"We just heard. The young man returned home. He had taken a different route home, apparently. Let's wrap this up."

Cal turned around and looked as if the sun was hiding behind the mountains and the clouds in the sky were all a brilliant orange.

"Hey Ligai, let's get a move on. We got a long drive ahead of us," Anderson said over the radio.

Cal picked up the pace. He was feeling good about getting out of the office and feeling good that the young man was okay and back at home.

It seemed a much faster return down the trail headed to the parking area. When Cal arrived, Anderson was in the cool pickup waiting for him.

"How far the hell did you go, boy?" Anderson asked.

"I made some good ground," Cal smiled as he snapped on his seat belt.

In an hour they were back at the sheriff's station as the brilliant orange sky had turned into a dark purple color. Cal made his way to his desk, where he saw a sticky note on his monitor. "The sheriff wants to speak with you".

Cal looked down the hallway to see if the sheriff was still in and saw the lights in his office were on, so he continued to his office and knocked on the open door.

"Ligai, come in. How's your first few weeks here?"

"Sir, I was glad to get into the field today. I'm ready to get out there," Cal replied.

"Yeah, I heard you went out with Anderson," the sheriff smirked. "Well, I finally have an assignment for you. We're assigning you to the patrol bureau, region B24. It's the south portion of the county."

"Thank you, sir. I'm very excited about this opportunity." Cal said as he went to shake the sheriff's hand.

"I know you'll do a fine job for us. I know you had a long day with Anderson. Report here in the morning. We'll have all the paperwork and information you'll need."

"Again, thank you, sir," Cal said and turned with a big smile. Not a bad day at all, he thought.

2

In the 1840s, the Peralta family from northern Mexico had developed rich gold mines in the Superstition Mountains. They routinely would bring their gold back to Mexico. In 1848, the international boundaries were being moved south of the Gila River due to the Mexican-American War. The Peralta family was bringing their final and largest load back to Mexico.

Over two dozen people, a good number of them members of the Peralta family, began their voyage home. The Apache Indians ambushed the Peralta group who were fleeing west. The Apache's forced them south, up against the Superstition Mountains, where the Mexicans were massacred. It was believed that a few of the miners from the Peralta group were able to escape.

It would be another twenty years until a patrol from Fort McDowell found the remains of over twenty-five people. No gold was found.[1]

* * *

The ten years had flown by for Cal Ligai. He had learned a lot about being assigned to the Patrol Bureau B24. His superiors and the other deputies help mold Cal into one of Pinal's finest. It wasn't to anyone's surprise when Cal applied for one of the Search and Rescue (SAR) coordinators in Pinal County.

He would be one of six deputy SAR coordinators in the county reporting to Sergeant Dale Melkin, a longtime veteran in the SAR unit. Two of the six SAR Coordinators would always be covering one of the largest counties in the state. Cal knew that a lot of time would be spent in the northern portion of the county, in the Superstition Mountains.

Cal seemed like a natural. He was always ready to help in search and rescue operations that occurred in Patrol Bureau B24, and he would volunteer for other missions. Cal had become an expert mountain climber and spent as much of his free time in the outdoor wilderness. He became a leader through an example to the other deputies and appeared to be headed up the fast track.

The sheriff of Pinal County tried to tell Cal he could move up the ladder faster in other positions. But Cal seemed to be drawn to this position, drawn to the Superstition Mountains. He still remembered one of his first weeks as a deputy, searching for a lost hiker in the same mountains his grandfather used to take him hiking in as a child.

It was a different type of position, and Cal had taken additional training to sharpen his skills in search and rescue. He had read numerous manuals inside and out. All this would lead to him acing the exam.

Cal was to report Monday morning to the Pinal County Sheriff's office in Florence. He spent the night before reviewing all the manuals he had studied for the exam. He knew Monday would be a full day spent with Dale Melkin. They had hit it off in the interview and Cal felt this was the type of person he could learn a lot from.

Monday morning came and Cal was one of the first people in the office. He grabbed some coffee and sat at one of the open desks. His head lifted each time someone entered the office.

"Good morning, Cal. Congratulations on your new position. I think you're a natural fit." Said an older woman as she headed down the hallway.

"Betty, thank you. I'm really excited about this opportunity." Cal replied.

"You better be," came a deep voice to Cal's right. Cal turned as Dale Melkin walked to his office. "Cal, give me about fifteen minutes, and then come to my office."

"Will do."

The next fifteen minutes seemed like an hour to Cal, who wanted to jump right into his new position.

Cal knocked on the open door. "Come on in Cal. Take a seat. I know you're probably keen to get started."

"Yes, sir," Cal replied as he sat across from the Sergeant.

"Well, I don't have to tell you about the job and the Superstitions. Per square foot, they are the most dangerous mountains in the world. Over six hundred people have died or gone missing in those mountains. And with more and more weekend warriors and all the treasure, Ligai, it's only getting worse."

"Yes, there is something about those mountains that draws people to them. My grandfather would take me hiking when I was younger. We came across numerous people injured or didn't bring enough water." Cal replied.

"As you know, there are forty SAR coordinators in the state, and many of them overlap in the Superstitions. I'm not sure if you've met Jose Rodríguez yet, but he will have the same shift as you. For the next month, I want you to ride with him. You'll cover both areas together." The Sergeant said.

"I've met him at a few search and rescue operations, but never had the opportunity to speak with him at any length," Cal replied.

"I've asked to stop over later and let the shadowing begin. You and I will meet on Friday afternoons to review your week and make sure there aren't questions or concerns. They won't be long. Jose should be able to answer everything along the way." The Sergeant got up and pulled a binder from the filing cabinet behind him.

The Sergeant continued, "We've got some training tomorrow afternoon. You've probably seen all this material but work with Jose to see what you can help with. As you're aware, the best chance for successful search and rescue is when we work with others. The trained volunteers, the SAR Posse, to assist with law enforcement, firefighters and national park services are all key. We've had FEMA, and the military involved as well. But again, it's the volunteers that are so critical. If they are trained properly, we have a better success rate."

"Yes. I'm familiar with the material and the importance of trained volunteers, sir. I'm sure I can be a help in the training." Cal replied as he saw from the corner of his eye someone enter the office.

"Jose', we were just talking about you," the Sergeant said as he stood up to shake the deputy's hand. "Have you met Cal?"

"I believe we have, but I think we were in the middle of a rescue. Not much time to talk," Jose said as he approached Cal as he stood and shook hands.

"You're right. A few times we worked together. The hiker who fell at Picacho Peak a few years back." Cal replied.

"Yep, I remember that one. He looked in terrible shape, but I believe he was fine." Jose said as he took a seat next to Cal.

The sergeant looked at Jose. "I want you to take Cal with you for a few weeks, then slowly give him his wings. Touch base daily at that point and see what happens. I'm sure we'll have a rescue or two in that time frame."

"Sounds good. I was thinking of having him meet some of the Tonto National Forest Rangers in the Supes as well. They are always such a great help." Jose said.

"Cal, we had almost seven hundred rescues last year across the state. Almost a hundred were in the Supes." the sergeant said.

Cal sat in the chair, itching to get out in the field. "I am up for the task. I'm looking forward to getting out there."

Jose stood up with a big smile. "Let's get him out of here and let's take a ride."

The two were driving up Route 79 in a short time.

"Cal, I've heard a lot of good things about you. If you like to be busy, the Supes will take care of that."

"Thanks. I do like to be busy. I kind of breathe, eat, and sleep my work." Cal said as he gazed out the window. The Supes were getting larger as they got closer.

"Single I'm guessing?" Jose chuckled.

"Yeah. I know my job is first and haven't found the right woman who would be good with that."

"Don't be in a hurry with this job. Especially covering the Supes. A few of the members of the team were drawn to the Superstition Wilderness, and the Search and Rescue, but the job can be intense, and the schedule can get crazy.

"Well, I'm not hoping for anything bad and anybody needing to be rescued, but I'm ready," Cal said.

Jose turned down Kings Ranch Road in Gold Canyon. "I want to point out the sheriff's depot here. It's one of the closer buildings to the mountains."

"Oh yeah, the one by the old burned-down movie studio," Cal replied.

"Movie studio, isn't that on Route 88 where they have the church from the Elvis movie?"

"They moved the church after the second fire. Nothing is there anymore."

Jose slowed down. "Well, here is the sheriff depot on the left. Where is this movie studio?"

"Just keep going, slowly. Right here behind the gate." Cal pointed to the east side of the street.

"Well, I didn't know that," Jose said with a big grin.

As he turned back to the highway, he pointed to the mountains. "The Cloudview trailhead to the left. You'll end up there, eventually." Jose laughed.

"I know that trailhead well. Hieroglyphs are there, although now rightly called the petroglyphs and the Lost Goldmine Trail." Cal replied. "You've got it. Pretty popular trailhead and we see a few broken ankles there throughout the year. The last few hundred yards to the petroglyphs seem to be the area where people twist an ankle."

"I've helped a few people back to the parking lot there," Cal said with a smile as he started feeling at home like he belonged. "What about Peak 5057?" He asked Jose.

"We've had our share of rescues there. Everyone wants to get to the highest point. If you've hiked it, you know it's not easy. That ten-foot-high technical climb for some hikers ends up with a helicopter ride."

"I can see that happening. I've climbed it a few times and think it's one of the more challenging hikes. But with any of them, steady and slow and stay hydrated."

"You got it, brother!"

As they made their way down Superstition Boulevard, Jose pointed to the mountains. "I'm guessing you've hiked up Flatiron?"

Flatiron was one of the most common strenuous hikes in the Superstitions. Its shape and flat top look like an old fashion iron to the people below. Most hikers entered the Dutchman State Park and headed up the siphon draw. That was the point where most people decided to turn around or climb up the very steep trail to the top.

"I have, several times."

"Be ready. You'll be bringing people down from there regularly. We had a group of fitness instructors from the east coast, climb up in the middle of summer."

Cal chuckled, "I remember that. Nothing prepared them for the desert heat in the summer and that mountain."

"You will see a lot of out-of-towners not familiar with the elements. The other group, although not as many, make the job more difficult are the treasure hunters." Jose said as he pulled into Dutchman's State Park.

"Yes, the legend of the Lost Goldmine is still alive, and people out there feel they'll be the ones to find it," Cal answered.

"I asked a few of the Tonto National Forest Rangers to meet us here. Shawn McTavish has been here for a few years. Seems to always be around when something is going on. I also asked Lil to meet us here. She is kind of a legend in the Tonto Forest. She probably knows the Superstition Wilderness better than anyone I ever met," Jose said as he pulled up to a Tonto Forest Rangers pickup truck in the parking lot.

A tall, fair complexion with dark red hair got out of one of the pickups. "That's McTavish."

"Shawn, Cal Ligai," Cal said as he got out of the vehicle to shake McTavish's hand.

"Pleasure to meet you. You'll be working on a few recoveries in no time, I'm sure."

Jose looked at the pickup. "Is Lil with you?"

"She should be here any minute. So, Cal, is this position a big change for you?" McTavish asked as he glanced at another Tonto Forest pickup truck making its way through the parking lot.

"Yes. But it's something I've wanted for some time, and I am really passionate about Search and Rescues. I've always tried to get involved with my other position for the county when it allowed. When I found out this was going to be opening up, it seemed like a no-brainer."

The other truck came to a stop and the three men watched as the small framed woman came out of the truck. She had dark straight hair and was of Native American heritage. In an instant, Cal recognized the ranger he had seen a decade back at Dutchman's State Park.

"Hey Lil, thanks for meeting us," Jose said as he greeted her with a handshake.

"No worries," as she turned to Cal. "Liluye Shanta. Just call me Lil. I believe we may have crossed paths years ago."

"Yes, I remember. You put Deputy Anderson in his place." Cal said as he shook her hand.

"That's me. Call it as I see it," she said with a smirk.

"Nothing wrong with that. I may rely on you on the terrain. I know you've been here for some time." Cal replied.

"I've been coming to these mountains since the time I could walk. I'll show you the hidden gems of the Superstition Wilderness," she said as she took a step back and acknowledged McTavish with a nod.

"Well, that's why I wanted you to meet Cal in person and ask you if you could each take him around with you for a day in the next month. Show him around. Lil, you know the terrain better than anyone." Jose asked the two rangers.

"Sure thing. How about next Wednesday?" she replied.

Jose turned to Cal, then back to Lil. "That should be fine. We are doing some training tomorrow and this will still give us a few days to go over everything. Shawn, maybe a few weeks down the road with you as well."

"Absolutely. A Thursday may be better for me, but when we get closer, I'll reach out to you guys," Shawn said as he looked at his calendar on the phone.

"I appreciate this. I've done some hiking up here but probably didn't look at the terrain the way I need to now," Cal replied.

Lil had gone to her truck and returned with a map and unfolded it on the hood of the pickup. "They don't make this version anymore, but Cal, I'll take you out to Peters Canyon. Bring a lot of water and comfortable shoes."

"Oh boy, it looks like Lil will be picking on you, Cal," Jose chuckled.

"I think you're right. She gave me a few months on the job before she took me there. It's as tough a hike as there is, and Lil seems to have her own trails. Get a good night's sleep the night before." Shawn added.

"Cal don't listen to them. It actually means I like you. I have a good feeling about you. I think you will grow to understand the powers of the Superstitions."

The next morning, Cal and Jose, with the help of a few other Deputy SAR Coordinators, worked with a dozen volunteers. He met Sheryl Gillen, another of the deputy SAR Coordinators in Pinal County who had a dozen years with their county sheriff department.

"Cal, welcome on board. I heard a lot about you, and I think you're going to fit in well with this team. You have some big shoes to fill, but I believe you'll get it done," Gillen said as she met Cal, as the volunteers were beginning to roll in.

The team and volunteers training headed out into the Superstitions to work on rope climbing. They were focusing on retrieving a person who may have fallen off a cliff or fallen into a deep crevice. For the next few hours, the team worked with all the volunteers and numerous techniques, including rappelling. Over the last few years,

Cal had become an expert climber and enjoyed sharing his knowledge with the volunteers. Cal knew it was also a great opportunity to review strengths and weaknesses with some volunteers.

Sheryl leaned over to Jose as they both observed the team from above as Cal was below, "Jose, this Cal is good. He's good with these people and an excellent teacher."

"I agree," Jose continued. "It's always a concern when you change up a team, but I like him. He's going to fit in nicely."

The session went longer than expected, as Cal wanted to make sure he could give individual attention to all the volunteers. By the time they all made it back to their vehicles, the sun was setting and gave the Superstitions a red hue. Cal was the last to leave, as he made sure everything was packed. He looked up at the mountains, taking in their beauty.

3

In the mid-1860s after the Civil War, Brevet Lieutenant John D Walker had made friends with the Pima Indians. He was placed in charge of neutralizing the Pima Indians' enemies, mainly the Apache and Yavapai. Walker led a group of Army infantry from Fort McDowell along with volunteers, and Pima scouts to attack the Apache and Yavapai camps throughout the Superstitions. In 1866 Walker's group killed over a dozen warriors at Hell's Hole and then continued up Tortilla Creek to Dismal Valley, killing another 57 Native Americans.

In the following two years, Walker led numerous attacks on the Apache and eliminated any threats from the Apache's going forward. Some twenty years later, John Walker lost his mind and died in California.[1]

* * *

Cal got an early drive out to the Tortilla trail head where Lil had asked him to meet her there. He had driven up route 88, out of Pinal County, past Canyon Lake, and took the road until the paved highway became a primitive road. Turning left at the fork would take him to Fish Creek Vista. Turning right would take you three and half-mile road, barely accessible with a 4 x4, to the trailhead.

Cal didn't see another truck and was happy to have arrived before Lil. He parked his truck and got out to stretch his feet. He took a drink of water and gazed at the mountains as the sun was almost on top of them.

"What took you?' came Lil's voice from behind him.

"I didn't see your truck. I didn't know you were here." Cal replied, a bit startled.

"First lesson of the Superstitions, there is much more in the mountains than what your eyes see," Lil said as she rearranged her backpack. "I hope you brought more than just that?" as she glanced at the water Cal was holding.

"Yes, I have a backpack in the truck."

"Great. Let's get started," she replied as she started heading north.

"Aren't we going down the trailhead to Peters Canyon?" Cal asked, pointing to the south.

"No, somewhere else. Are you ready?" Lil asked and turned, not waiting for Cal to answer.

The two continued walking up the dirt road that Cal had arrived on. Soon they approached an old metal tank, the slab, and an old stone water tank.

"Cal, have you ever been here?' Lil said as her eyes continued northward.

"No, I don't believe so," he said as his eyes followed Lil's glare.

"This is Tortilla Well. Not functioning, of course," as she lifted her hand and pointed up the trail. "We're going to Tortilla Ranch. From there we'll follow the creek until we get to Tortilla Creek Waterfalls. It's actually the back way, as most people come from the West."

"That sounds great," Cal replied.

"See, I told you, I'm taking you here because I like you," she said with a smirk as her eyes met his.

Soon they arrived at the remains of Tortilla Ranch. Some concrete slabs, an old stone water tank, some old troughs, and metal poles.

"So they say this was part of the Reavis Ranch operation at one time," Lil said as she stop to take a drink.

"I've been out to the Reavis Ranch years ago. I didn't realize the scope of their operation."

"It was some good land, so the cattle company wanted it. Prior to that, my people farmed this area." Lil replied. "Some call it Dismal Valley."

"Yes. A lot of Native American tribes lived in the Superstitions. My grandmother was part Native American. She died before I was born, but my grandfather spoke of her frequently."

Lil looked at him with a grin. "I thought maybe when I first met you."

The two followed the creek downstream until they hit the waterfall area. The falls were just a trickle as the water fell fifty feet.

"Lil, that's pretty impressive. It looks like a few people climbed down to the bottom from here," as he pointed to an area that seemed to be clear.

"Yes. We're going down and off the trail. I'm taking you to Hell's Hole."

Cal looked up at the steep rocks and started scrambling down them. "Well, you have me motivated," he chuckled as he moved cautiously to the next boulder. When he made his way to the bottom, he turned and reached his arm up to help Lil.

Lil took another drink, "Cal, I can see you're an expert climber and in good shape.

Cal couldn't help but smirk but as Lil saw it appear on his face, "You'll need it to keep up with me." and the smirk disappeared.

Cal sipped some water as he looked at the drawings on the rocks in front of them. "My grandfather would always tell me what the pictures meant," as he looked closer at the one in front of him, "This one looks familiar."

Lil looked at the drawing, "Yes, this is a common theme you'll see in the mountains." She pointed out the two hunters, a darker brown in color than the rock, multiple longhorn sheep, and a large sun over to the side. On top of all of them looked to be a large white hunter overlooking all the other figures.

Cal pointed to the larger hunter. "I assume he is in charge?"

"I guess you could say that. He depicts a great warrior. As the story goes, he oversees the people in the Superstitions to make sure their way of life is safe." Lil replied.

"Yep, I think my grandfather had told me that story."

The two continue hiking through the riverbed. Lil would point out drawings along the way and what they may have represented.

It was tedious as they maneuvered through numerous boulders and pools of water. After some time, Lil stopped, sloping hills on both sides. To the north was the higher elevation.

"This is Hell's Hole," Lil lifted her arm and pointed in all directions. "This is where some of my ancestors were attacked and killed in the 1860s by a group from Fort McDowell. They continued down the path we came from to Dismal Valley killing over 50 Apache, including women and children."

"Dismal Valley, by Tortilla Ranch? I remember you calling it when we were there," Cal asked.

"Yes. A lot of death in these mountains. A lot of ghosts."

The two continued back to the riverbed they had taken out. Lil continued to point out drawing and took a small excursion to show Cal a small ruin. As they got closer to the primitive road Cal had taken to get to the trailhead, Lil led him north.

"I'm parked up near the Tortilla trailhead. I can drive you to your truck then," Lil said.

Although it was a long day of hiking, the day went by fast. He enjoyed learning about the Superstition's history and spending time with Lil.

"Lil, are you hungry? You do eat?" he smiled. "Can I buy you dinner at Tortilla Flat?"

"Yes, I eat. I eat a lot! And yes, you can," she smiled back at him.

Lil dropped Cal off at his truck and then they headed back to route 88 to Tortilla Flat. The town started in the early 1900s as a stagecoach stop. Today it's a handful of buildings with a population of as little as six people in any given year.

Lil pulled into town first and found an open parking spot while Cal found it a bit more challenging. Although small, it is a frequent destination for both locals to the region and visiting tourists.

By the time Cal found a parking spot, Lil had made it into the restaurant and got a table for both of them. Cal made his way past the bar that had saddles for seats and headed to the far corner where Lil was.

"I got us a table," Lil continued, "Sometimes there is a wait," she smiled.

"You got lucky," Cal said as he surveyed the room. The walls were covered with one-dollar bills and had such a nostalgic feel of the old West. "This hasn't changed much. It still looks like it did when my grandfather would take me."

"Yes, I like history. This place has a lot of it. I don't think we should ever forget about our past," Lil replied.

A waitress came and left some menus and left them a few glasses of water. "Lil, do you come here often?"

"A few times a year. If I have a special guest or I know it's a place a person I know would enjoy," Lil said.

"Which one am I," Cal joked.

"I think you are both, Cal."

"So Lil, you're a Tonto Ranger and you volunteer for search and rescue operations in your free time?" Cal asked.

"Yes. Besides that, I guess I don't have much of a life," Lil laughed.

Cal smiled a took a sip of his water. "I really appreciate you taking me out into the Superstitions. Everyone told me you know the terrain better than anyone out here."

"It's home. Literally and figuratively. I grew up in these mountains and this is where my ancestors have been for hundreds of years."

"I remember my grandfather showing me a lot of history and the drawings." Cal paused. "The drawings were important to him. Honestly, I don't remember a lot of them. I was young, but now I remember him pointing out the large white warrior. Like the one you showed me."

"He knew of the importance of it," Lil replied.

"I guess so. That white warrior protects your people all those years ago." Cal continued as he gazed through the menu. "My grandfather used to tell me about the Thunder God protecting the Superstitions as well."

"Yes, the Thunder God has protected my people. Actually, the White Warrior has yet to show, but he will be here when the people of the Superstitions are in need of protection. That's the story at least," Lil said as the waitress came to take their order.

For the next hour, the two shared some stories of their experiences in the mountains as they ate and had a beer. "Well, Cal, I know we both are working tomorrow and we," Lil scanned the bar, "have a long drive to get home."

"Yes. Thank you. I'll take care of the bill, and I know we'll be talking frequently." Cal said as he stood as Lil stood and walked to the exit. Cal had a good feeling about things to come.

For the next few weeks, Cal rode with Deputy Rodriguez. They had a few calls ranging from a hiker with a twisted ankle on the Picketpost Mountain Trail, heavy rain causing some flash flooding with a vehicle stuck in the flooding to a car rolling down an embankment on Route 60.

Jose took Cal to meet the Air and Rescue team stationed at Williams Field and Cal attended a virtual meeting with county and state SAR Coordinators. His Friday meeting with the Sheriff was brief, just as the Sheriff had thought.

Things were going as expected and the wings were finally cut. Cal was on his own. It was a Friday night, and Cal felt like it was something to celebrate. He picked up his phone and went through his contacts, then placed his phone back on the seat, started the car, and started home.

He was stopped at a signal light and looked up at the magnificent orange and red sunset. He picked up his phone and went to his contacts and dialed.

"Hello Lil, it's Cal. Are you doing anything tonight?"

* * *

The next day a call came in, a missing hiker, last known to be going up to Massacre Falls. Cal was at the Depot in Gold Canyon and quickly responded to the dispatch.

"I'll be at First Water in 15 minutes. Have anyone available to meet me at the Crosscut Trailhead? Dispatch the airfield and let's get some eyes in the sky. We're running out of daylight."

Within ten minutes Cal had turned up the primitive road known as First Water. Cal maneuvered around the large potholes. His memory flashed ten years back when he and Deputy Anderson helped to look for a lost hiker. As Cal's Search and Rescue truck turned into the parking area for the trailhead, he remembered it was the first time he met Lil. As he came to a stop, he saw a Tonto Ranger truck and Lil getting out of it.

"Lil, are you able to assist?" Cal asked.

"You got me for the search. When I heard there was a search, I quickly made sure with my supervisor I could help." Lil answered.

"Lil, you are fast, I'll give you that." Cal smiled as he started spreading out a map on the hood of his truck. He saw the helicopter on the horizon and knew they would start with a standard sweep of the area. Additional vehicles pulled in, including a deputy, and a half a dozen volunteers.

"Thank you, everyone, for coming out. We're looking for an 18-year-old white male, Bob Kravis. He went out this morning to the Massacre Grounds, and that's all we know. His father said he didn't appear to have more than a few liters of water and he told his dad he wouldn't be gone long. He was wearing an orange short-sleeve shirt and tan shorts. This afternoon his mother called us that he had not returned yet. In this heat and if he really only had a few liters, we need to move quickly. Could be he twisted his ankle and is waiting for us."

Cal adjusted the map. "Okay, looks like we're ten of us and have eyes above. This is where I wanted each of you," Cal began showing the areas he wanted the team to fan out as they all headed to the Massacre Grounds.

The last assignment was for Lil, "Lil, you and I will take the lead on the main trail." Lil's eyes met Cal's, and she nodded in agreement.

The team quickly went up the trail and slowly split into different segments. Lil and Cal kept a fast pace. They could hear the team calling out for Bob.

Lil was looking down at the trail. "A lot of fresh marks here. If he was on the trail, someone would have stumbled across him," she said to Cal.

"Yes, I noticed that. He may have deviated from the trail and then could have fallen. Possibly laying anywhere."

"Besides the Falls themselves, there are a few spots where we've had some hikers stumbling down a ridge," Lil said.

Cal got on the radio. "Anything, anyone." Just followed by a few negatives. "It looks like there were numerous hikers out here recently. Make sure you're checking any area where someone could have slipped or fallen off. Rescue One, do you see anything from up there?"

"Negative Cal. Just a few hikers moving up the trail," came the voice from the helicopter.

Lil and Cal continued up the trail, getting to a higher elevation. Lil stopped to take a drink and pointed to the rocks up to the left. "There is a famous photo area where we've seen a few people fall. Let's take a look," as she started up at an even faster pace.

Cal continued to survey all the land on both sides, looking for an orange shirt. Lil came to the ridge and looked down and called out. She scanned the area around. "Okay, let's check out the Falls."

"I'm right behind you," Cal said

Within twenty minutes they came to Massacre Falls, although this time of year it was just a trickle. The area had numerous large boulders and crevasses, all of which could conceal a person.

Cal came across a similar drawing of hunters, longhorn sheep etched in the rocks in a reddish color, while a large white warrior stood above them all. Cal took a drink and surveyed the area.

"Bob. Bob, can you hear us?" Cal yelled out as he and Lil spread out, checking the area.

After another twenty minutes, the two check the area. Lil climbed a few boulders near the falls to get a better view, but the two were coming up empty.

Lil looked at Cal, "Maybe the others will have better luck,"

"Maybe, but we would have heard something by now."

Cal reached out to the team on the radio, but no one had anything to report. "Lil, let's head east. Maybe he went on."

Lil nodded in agreement. "Yep, it's always the next ridge. One more."

The two climbed up the ridge to the east. At the top, Cal scanned the area with his binoculars, but all he saw were a few longhorn sheep.

"Cal," came the voice of the pilot of the helicopter, "Just came in. The boy is fine. At home, all is good."

"Great, thank you for the news," Cal said as he turned to Lil. "Well, I guess it's a good outcome. It seems to happen a few times where they ended up at home."

Lil smiled back "Now and then, not that common."

"Same thing ten years ago. Well, it's a good outcome," Cal grinned.

The two turned back down the trail and headed to the trailhead parking lot.

4

In 1865, Dr. Abraham Thorne was working at Fort McDowell, 30 miles from the Superstitions. Thorne treated the sick Apache on their reservation and earned respect from their leaders.

The Apache wanted to reward Thorne for his services and blindfolded Thorne for twenty miles, taking him to a gold mine. He was told he could take as much gold as he could carry. He came back to the Fort and sold the ore for $6,000.

He was set on finding the mine again. He got a few of his friends together. Some say he found the mine again, others say he didn't. Either way, he never made it alive out of the Superstition Mountains.[1]

* * *

The next week was quiet. A few hikers ran into some minor issues, but nothing significant. Cal used this opportunity to meet with as many of the volunteers as possible. It almost always came down to manpower when looking for lost hikers.

Most of them appreciated the reach out and discussed successes.

Cal sensed a strong passion and competitiveness with Waylen Cambria. He had been volunteering for years, searching for lost hikers. He had a reputation for never giving up and going beyond what others could do.

Waylen said all the right things and had an impressive record, but Cal thought there was a part of him he still needed to get to know.

The two had met at a local coffee shop and Waylen quickly went in. He was one of the most experienced people in the Superstitions.

"Deputy Ligai, your predecessor, Jose, and frankly, most of the deputies don't take advantage of my expertise. For some reason, everyone likes to think that little ranger who volunteers with us knows more," Cambria rambled.

"Are you speaking of Lil Shanta?" Cal asked, already knowing the answer.

"Yeah. Because she's a ranger they think she knows the Superstitions better than anyone else. Sometimes people act like we don't know them as well. Trust me, I know it very well."

"I plan on evaluating people on what I see firsthand. That's all I can tell you," Cal replied.

"That's fair. Take it as friendly advice, spread the work around," Cambria said with a smirk.

For the next half hour, they spoke mainly on the logistics of situational rescues. Cal knew Cambria knew his stuff, but appeared he was in competition with Lil. He wondered what Lil's view of Cambria was. It could be best to keep them apart. While it was fresh and quiet, he figured he'd text Lil to see if she was free this evening to meet for a beer.

Lil had mentioned a small rundown pub in Apache Junction. She said she could meet him there at 6 PM. Cal ended up getting there a little early and picked out two stools at the far end of the bar.

Cal sipped his beer, watching the people in the bar while keeping one eye on the door, waiting for Lil. Cal got a few looks from a few shady characters, as he was still in his uniform.

He took the last sip of his beer when he heard the front door of the pub crash closed. He turned in and saw Lil making her way over to him.

Lil placed her hand on Cal's shoulder as she propped herself up on the stool. "These stools aren't made for us short people," she joked. "So, thank you for the invite."

"Well, you mentioned if I need your help, so…" Cal said with a smile as he lifted his hand to get the bartender's attention.

"Here I thought it was a social invite," Lil smiled back and then told the bartender who was approaching "Chuck, my regular."

Cal responded quickly, "It's two-pronged. I get information and I get it from someone I enjoy spending time with."

Lil placed his hand on his shoulder, "I'm just busting your balls."

Cal laughed, turning to the bartender. "Same as last one," then turned to Lil and said, "It's true, I appreciate your help and enjoy your company."

"Okay, before this gets any more awkward, what can I help you with?" Lil responded as she took a sip of her beer.

"Well, I met with a lot of the volunteers over the last week," Cal continued. "It seemed to go over well."

"Yeah, I would assume so. They need a little stroking now and then. Good for you."

"Lil, what can you tell me about Waylen Cambria?"

"Good old Waylen. He actually is a good guy and means well. He just isn't good with people and wants to do his own thing." Lil responded.

"That's the feeling I got, but that could be a recipe for a disaster," Cal said as a smile came across his face.

"What? Did I say something funny?" Lil asked.

"No, sorry," Cal's face became more serious. "Anything happened in the past that may have jeopardized a rescue, or it became a bit disorganized?"

"No, he'll throw his two cents in, even when he shouldn't, but in the end, he does a good job over covering the terrain of the Supes. He's just a very competitive guy."

"Okay, good to know. So, no issues working with him?" Cal said.

"None at all. What else? Next question." She snapped back.

"That's it," Cal said.

"So maybe you weren't bullshitting me that you like my company," she said, smiling at Cal.

The two sat at the bar most of the evening, picking each other's brains, sharing stories, and laughing. As the pub emptied, Lil looked at the clock on the wall. "Cal, I need to be at the Peralta Trailhead first thing in the morning. Let me get this," she said as she got herself off the stool.

"No, I have this," Cal replied.

"Are you sure? Maybe I can pay half?" she said as Cal stood from his stool.

"You get the next one." Cal smiled at her.

Lil placed her hand on Cal's chest and reached over to kiss him on the cheek. "Confident there will be a next time, are we?" She then headed for the door as Cal closed out the bill with the bartender.

* * *

Sarah and Jennifer felt the scorching sun on their shoulders as they made their way to Fremont Saddle. There they had a magnificent site of Weavers Needle. The girls were seniors and wanted to take advantage of the day off from school.

"Sarah, thanks for suggesting this. I know I slowed you down, but I think I did better than our 'friends" who didn't make it," Jennifer said as she focused her camera on Weavers Needle.

"You did well Jen.   Going down will be a little easier. We did some good elevation, I think 1300 feet," Sarah said. "We were a bit slow on the way up. The last time I made it here was in about 90 minutes."

"Oh wow, I'm sorry. I must have slowed you down," Jennifer replied.

"No worries. It's always fun to see some of these trails with people who are experiencing it for the first time." Sarah said as she drank some water and pulled out some mixed nuts from her backpack. "Here, have some of these before we go down," as she handed the bag to Jennifer.

Jennifer sat on one boulder as she overlooked the Superstitions.   "Sarah, can you imagine the first explorers? Such a different place."

"Really. Weavers Needle was named after one of those explorers, Pauline Weaver. I think he was a scout." Sarah said as she adjusted her backpack. "Ready to go down?"

"Sure," as Jennifer stood up and looked back down the canyon, the two spent hours hiking up.

The first few hundred yards were switchbacks, and Jennifer was happy that they were easier going down. Sarah got a few chuckles as Jennifer would tell the people they passed who were headed up, "Only a few more minutes, you're almost there!"

The two could appreciate the spectacular rock formations of Peralta Canyon. Jennifer looked at the horizon as Sarah picked up the pace.

"Wow," Jennifer said as she felt her feet slip and heard the stones rumble below her feet. At the last minute, she regained her balance, stopping herself from falling.

Sarah quickly turned back, "Are you okay?" As she could see Jennifer regained her balance. "Keep your eyes on the trail. If you want to look and take a picture or two, we can stop."

"Yeah, sorry. It's incredible up here. I bet I can get one of these pictures in the school newsletter," as she held her camera up.

The two continued down the switchbacks of the canyon. Jennifer kept one eye on the path and another on the scenery of the canyon. She turned as she heard stones fall from the cliff to her right side. She swung her head up and thought she saw something along the top.

"I think there is someone up there," she called out to Sarah, and she held up her camera and zoomed quickly, and began to take pictures.

Sarah turned to her friend and then focused her eyes on the top of the cliff high above. "I don't see anyone. There might be someone up there, but there sure isn't a path that I know of."

"I think it was a person," as she reviewed the photos in the digital viewer. "It's so hard to see in this little viewer in the bright sunshine. I bet when I get home and download it and blow it up, I'll get a good view," she said as she continued to view the photos. "Yep, definitely a person, but hard to make out. How cool."

"Well, now we have a reason to pick up the pace," Sarah said, getting frustrated by her friend stopping continually.

Periodically Jennifer would stop to take additional pictures. Sarah continued down the trail with a quicker stride as she heard stones sliding from under her feet. She turned to see Jennifer had fallen.

"Are you all right?" Sarah said as she knelt by her friend.

Tears trickled down Jennifer's face as she tried to stand and pick up her camera that had tumbled to the rocks. "I think I twisted my ankle and my wrist, well, I fell on it," Jennifer cried harder. "My camera, it looks broken," as she hobbled to pick it up.

"Here I got it," Sarah said as she went to retrieve the camera. "Can you make it down? Maybe if I help you? I can run down to the trailhead and see if anyone is there?"

"Maybe if you help me," Jennifer sobbed harder as she took the broken camera from Sarah.

The two slowly went down the trail as they were passed by numerous hikers going down.

"Are you guys okay? Do you need help? Should I see if the ranger is still at the entrance?" One hiker said as they passed by.

Sarah turned to Jennifer and then to the hiker. "I think we are okay for now. Thanks."

The two continued down the path, taking breaks every ten minutes. "Jen, just sit here for a few minutes. Drink a little water, we're almost there."

The sun was rising in the sky and the temperature was climbing. Sarah held back from drinking her thermos, as she knew Jennifer had already finished hers because of the frequent stops.

"Okay, let me help you to your feet," Sarah said as she lifted Jennifer and placed her arm around Sarah. As the two got more tired, it became more difficult.

"Sarah, I'm sorry. I should have been watching where I was going," as the two struggled, almost losing their feet.

At that point, the two girls heard a voice from farther down the path. "Hold on, I'm almost there. Take a seat."

The two girls sat on a large boulder as a young female ranger approached them.

"I'm Ranger Shanta." Lil untied Jennifer's boot and examined it. "It looks like your ankle is pretty swollen. Can you put any weight on it? Lil asked Jennifer.

"No, not really. My parents are going to kill me if you have to send me in a helicopter." Jennifer cried.

"Don't worry." Lil looked at Sarah. "what's your name?"

"I'm Sarah and this is Jennifer."

"Sarah, are you okay to take her on one side and I'll take the other?

"Yes, that would be a lot easier than what we were doing," Sarah replied.

Lil looked at the camera that Jennifer was clutching onto. "Okay, I'll take the camera for now. Let me have your backpack as well." As Lil placed both in her large backpack.

The three continued down the trail at a reasonable pace.

"Okay, girls, when you get home, I'd see about going to the emergency room," Lil said as they got to the parking lot. "Is your vehicle here?"

"Yes, the old black pickup," Sarah pointed. "Over there."

The three made their way to the pickup as Lil and Sarah helped Jennifer into the back seat, where she could extend her leg.

"I need to fill out some paperwork. Can you wait here a minute? My truck is around the corner." Lil said as she left the two girls. As she made her way to her truck, she took Jennifer's backpack and camera out of hers. She examined both and got her tablet out and walked back to the girls.

Lil continued to get information from the girls. "I think I have everything," as Lil looked at Sarah. "Your friend needs to see a doctor. You understand that, correct?"

"Yes," Sarah replied. "Thank you for your help."

Lil turned, and she heard the girl's pickup truck back away and leave down the primitive road. She then looked to the canyon as she scanned the top of the ridge.

* * *

Cal sat at his desk, finishing up his weekly reports and thinking about the safety program they were putting together for hikers. His mind turned to the young man they had been looking for earlier in the month when he first got this position. His family had called that evening that he returned home.

He knew the scenario had played out twice for him. The first time was a decade earlier when he first became a deputy. Maybe the young man would have some insight on losing his way while hiking alone and advice to share. He wondered if it would be interesting to speak with him. He pulled the report from the file, Bob Kravis. No phone number was in the report, so he wrote the address and headed for the truck.

The Kravis family lived in Mesa, Arizona, fifteen minutes from the Superstitions. It was in the next county, Maricopa, but it had been quiet for a few days and wasn't that far from Superstitions if Cal received a call over the radio.

Within a half hour, he pulled in front of a tired ranch home. As Ligai made his way to the front door, he could feel the blistering sun that would slowly settle, baking on his back.

He knocked on the door and a small framed man with gray hair came to the door. "Mr. Kravis," Cal said.

"Yes," the man returned as he coughed nervously.

"Deputy Cal Ligai from the Pinal Search and Rescue." Cal continued.

"Oh, yes, come on in," the man said as he opened up the wooden screened door to let Cal in.

The man pointed his cane at the couch. "Deputy, can I get you anything to drink?" he said as he gestured for Cal to take a seat in the living room.

"No Thank you," Cal replied.

"Well, it's awfully good of you to come out to see personally to speak with me."

"I'm really here about Bob," Cal said as he said on the couch.

"Any news?" the man said as he became excited.

"News? I was wondering if I could speak with him." Cal said, confused.

The man's expression transformed. "What kind of games are you playing? I got numerous calls that you would continue to look for him."

Cal stood up. "From who?"

"You Deputy Ligai. Are you going to tell me you don't remember any of the calls? At least three of them," the man said as his voice was becoming angry.

"I'm sorry, Mr. Kravis, that wasn't me, I can assure you."

"Look, you told me the search would continue, and now you act like he should be home. This is sick. Are you telling me you haven't been looking for him?"

"Mr. Kravis, on the day of the search, we got a call from you or some family member that Bob returned home."

The man sat on the couch and placed his head in his hands. "This is like some bad dream."

"Mr. Kravis, I can only imagine how difficult this is. When you received the calls, the person said it was me?" Cal said as he pulled a small pad out and started writing down information.

"Yes. On the first call you said we will continue to search and you would call me every week, which you have," the man replied.

"Were you given a phone number by any chance?' Cal asked.

"Yes, let me see. It's somewhere here. I never called it as you," the man paused, "or someone called every week." As the man passed the paper with the phone number on.

Cal quickly dialed the number, but there was no answer on the other end.

"Mr. Kravis. If you get another call, I want you to contact me right away. We will start looking for your son immediately, and second, I will find out who called you."

5

The Lost Dutchman and his gold are synonymous with the Superstition Mountains. A good portion of the hundreds of deaths over the last one-hundred and twenty-five years is due to finding the uncovering of the Dutchman goldmine. In the 1870s, Jacob Waltz, the Dutchman, who was actually German, was said to have located a gold mine in the Superstitions.

For years Jacob Waltz would pay for goods and services with gold nuggets. Many people tried to follow him from Phoenix to the Superstitions, hoping to find his gold mine. The Dutchman could always lose those who followed him.

In the Fall of 1891, Jacob Waltz became deathly ill. Julia Thomas, a local woman, was taking care of Jacob, and upon his deathbed, he described the location of his mine, to Julia. A lot of it made little sense and she looked with the help of others for years to no avail.

Some believe that Jacob Waltz had not found the lost gold mine but rather had found saddlebags from the mules that carried the gold and had scattered when the Peralta's were massacred.

Since his death, hundreds of men and women have searched for the truth, many paying with their lives.[1]

* * *

Cal drove back to the sheriff's station in Florence and sat at his desk, waiting for the sheriff to call him back. What a cluster. How could this have happened? He looked at the notes. Deputy Garcia from the Maricopa Sheriff's Department stopped at the home the next morning to speak with Mr. Kravis and his son Bob. He jotted down Deputy Garcia's number. Probably the next call after he spoke with the sheriff.

What else bothered Cal was someone was calling the Kravis family, claiming to be him. Who would do that and why? Was the protocol followed correctly? It appeared to be, but maybe they missed something. Lil had told him it happens now and then.

He opened reports on the computer and filtered hikers. Thousands of reports, what would the next filter be? Cal then thought of the first weeks as a deputy and a similar situation occurred. He plugged in the date. There it was, Michael Kowalski. Cal looked at it on the monitor, but his eyes were tired. He sent it to the printer and went to retrieve it.

Cal's phone rang, and it was the sheriff. He pulled out the notes and explained the situation to the sheriff. The next morning, another recovery search would take place in the Superstitions and a missing persons bulletin would go out. As the sheriff said, it could be someone running away to start a new life. He also agreed with Cal to call Deputy Garcia in the morning.

Tomorrow was going to be a long day, and he was going to see if Mr. Kravis would give them permission to record another potential call coming in claiming to be Cal. Cal dialed Jose as he wanted to see what Jose may know. It went straight to voicemail.

Cal leaned back in his chair and noticed the clock on the wall. Ten after eleven, time to go home and get some sleep. He wanted to get Lil two cents on this but at this time of the night, it would be best to wait till the morning.

The next morning Cal called Lil on his way to the trailhead, filling her in on all the details. The young man was still missing. A sheriff spoke with the family and a young man the next day. And someone was calling the family, identifying themselves as him.

"Cal, that makes no sense. I'm on my way to the trailhead now," Cal's phone rang as another call was coming in, Deputy Garcia.

"Okay, thanks, I have a call coming in. I'll see you in a bit."

"Hello Cal Ligai," Cal answered, knowing it was Deputy Garcia.

"Hey, Deputy Garcia, I got your message this morning. You wanted to know about the Kravis family," came a calm voice over the phone.

"Yes, thanks for calling back. Just checking up on the Kravis family. You saw them the next day. Anything peculiar?"

"Nothing out of the ordinary. They seemed embarrassed about all the fuss," the deputy replied.

"And the son Bob, did you speak with him?"

"Yes, apologized. Said he stopped at a friend's home and his cell phone had died. Is there a problem?" the deputy said, as his inflection changed.

"There could be," Cal replied. "Did you give him a number to call if there were questions?"

"Well, I handed him a card when I introduced myself. That's it. He placed it in his pocket. He looked like he was on his way to work, seemed like he was in a hurry. I believe he said that he and his son were going to help the neighbor with landscaping."

"Landscaping? I'd be surprised if he could do that. When I met him yesterday, he was using a cane and appeared quite frail." Cal replied.

"No cane, and he was a big guy. The kind of guy you want with you in a dark alley."

"Really? When I met Mr. Kravis last night, a small guy with gray hair and used a cane."

"Not the same guy I met. Again, a big guy with jet-black hair. What's going on?" the deputy asked with a bit of an edge.

"I stopped over last night to check on the family and Bob never came home that day and, as you said, we spoke to a different person. He also received numerous calls from someone claiming to be me." Cal replied.

"What? That's crazy. All I can tell you is I spoke to a father and son who said they were the Kravis's. No need to think otherwise," the deputy said defensively.

"Oh, I agree. Well, we are searching for the boy again and have a bulletin out on Bob Kravis as missing. When you get a second, check the photo and let me know if it was the same kid you spoke to."

"Will do," the deputy said as the phone went dead.

Cal made his way down Highway 88 and turned down the First Water dirt road leading to the trailhead. The search for Bob Kravis in the Superstitions was now a recovery one.   Cal met Jose and volunteers, including Waylen and Lil, in the Massacre Falls trailhead parking lot. Everyone had their assignments, and Cal and Lil took the main path.

"Lil, I'm not sure how this could have happened. How many times do you get a call about a lost hiker in the Supes, and then a call later that they are safe and home?" Cal said as they scanned the trail as they moved forward.

"Cal it happens. Maybe once a year, I guess. The first time we met that happened," she replied.

"Yep, I remember," Cal replied. "But with this, we followed up with the family. Deputy Garcia from the Maricopa Sheriff's Department. He said when he went there, he spoke to the father and the son. On top of that, someone has been calling them, identifying themselves as me. What the hell is going on?"

"I agree. Something doesn't add up. I'm sure it will all come together," Lil said as she took a step to the side looking down at a ravine. "One thing at a time, let's find this kid."

"Hopefully, the bulletin released this morning will find that he is somewhere safe and alive. We know if we find him in the mountains, he'll be dead."

The two continued for the next few hours, hiking up to Massacre Falls and beyond. Cal stayed in touch with the team of deputies, rangers, and volunteers as they all combed the mountain.

Cal looked up at the helicopter as it made several passes over the area. Cal got on the radio. "Why don't we all move fifty yards north, as we head back to the trailhead?" He knew it was a tight grid and if the young man was in this area, someone should come across the body.

Another few hours, with some chatter on the radio, but no sign of the hiker. As the two saw the partial group at the trailhead, Cal turned to Lil. "Did we do the calculations correctly? If he did hike this trail that morning, how far could he have gone?"

"Cal, from what I saw, you had the area covered. Maybe he's somewhere far from this mountain. Somewhere safe with friends," Lil replied, not believing what she said.

"Let's hope. Now who did Deputy Garcia speak with? And who is calling as me? Too much weird shit."

As the remainder of the team gathered around Cal, he gave them new trails on the chance he changed his mind that morning.

"Make sure you have enough water and stay in contact." Cal turned to Lil, "You up for Flatiron?"

The next week several teams, including state, county, and local volunteers, searched throughout the Superstitions looking for Bob Kravis. Cal had placed Lil in charge of the team, looking in some of the remote areas of the Superstitions, as she was the most knowledgeable. The air was covered by the search and rescue helicopters as well as the National Guard. After a week, hope turned to Bob Kravis showing up in some other town and not in the Superstitions as no one could last a week without water in this environment.

*   *   *

Sarah wasn't too happy that if she wanted to go hiking, she had to take her younger brother. With the experience she had with her friend Jennifer, her parents were adamant that neither one of their children hiked the mountains alone. Spring was here and Sarah wanted to get as much hiking in before summer, so she had very little choice unless she found someone else to go hiking with.

Sarah pulled into the parking lot of the trailhead in her old pickup truck her father had given her and turned to her brother as she put the truck into park. "Freddy, okay remember for the first part of the hike, keep your eyes open for the SD card that fell out of Jennifer's camera. I don't think we'll find it, but I said we would look for it."

"Yeah, I remember. It has a bright yellow label on it," he said as he got out of the truck and looked up at the mountain.

"Do not get ahead of me. If you wanted me to take you again, I expect you to stay close and listen."

"Okay, yeah, I'm just excited. You're the boss," he said as the two opened the gate to the trail.

The two headed up the trail, both with backpacks and water. Freddy fixed his eyes on the ground, looking for a small yellow SD card from Jennifer's camera. He knew his sister was right. They had little chance of finding it yet he continued to look on the edges of the trail.

"Here it is," said Sarah.

"The SD card?" Freddy turned to his sister.

"No. This is where Jennifer fell," Sarah continued. "Let's just take a few minutes to comb the area."

"Sure," her brother replied.

The two looked around, turning over small rocks and shuffling the stones.

"Okay, we tried," Sarah said as she continued up the trail.

"Yep, works for me," replied Freddy.

"I love this trail, but I was just on it," Sarah said after a few hundred feet.

"Well, let's hike off the trail," Freddy said as he turned off what seemed to be a small trail.

"Freddy, that's not a good idea," she said, following her brother.

"It looks like someone had been here. Let's see where it leads." Freddy replied.

The canyon walls seemed to close in on them as they proceeded down the trail they found. Sarah kept looking over her shoulder.

"I have this feeling we are not alone on this trail," Sarah said.

"I'm sure there are some others on here. The trail seems to be used a bit," Freddy said as he looked up at the steep cliff.

"No. I mean, like someone is watching us," she replied to her brother.

"Maybe a snake is watching you," Freddy chuckled. As he said that, he came to a crack in the canyon wall and went over to check it out.

"Freddy, get over here," Sarah yelled, but it was too late as Freddy turned the corner and was out of sight.

When Freddy turned up into the natural crevice of the canyon wall, he was stunned to see a boy about his age. The boy stood and looked at Freddy.

"Oh, you startled me," Freddy said to the boy as he stood for a minute. The boy waved and then ran off farther into the hidden trail.

"Freddy, get over here," his sister continued to yell as she appeared around the corner.

"I just saw someone. He took off. I think I scared him," Freddy said.

"You scared me. Come on, back to the main path." Sarah said as her brother followed.

The two continued up to Fremont Saddle, neither one saying much. They stopped several times along the way for water, but quickly began moving again.

Once at the top, Freddy turned to his sister. "I'm wondering who he was with. I didn't see anyone with him."

"Like you! You took off and were by yourself," she replied.

"Yes. Okay."

The two went back down the trail to Sarah's truck. Instinctively, they both searched the area where Jennifer had fallen, but again found nothing.

At the trailhead, Sarah noticed a ranger there. She thought it was Ranger Shanta. As she and her brother got closer, Sarah could recognize that it was her.

"I'm not sure if you remember me," Sarah said to Lil and continued. "You helped my friend last week on this trail. She hurt her ankle."

"Of course. How is your friend doing?" Lil replied.

"Better, although no hiking for a bit. I was wondering if you came across an SD card for a camera. My friend Jen, her camera. Well, the SD card must have fallen out." Sarah said.

"You know, I think I have it. Do you know if it was yellow?"

"Yep, it is," Sarah replied enthusiastically.

"It must have fallen out when I placed it in the truck. Let me go get it," Lil said as she walked over to the truck and came back with the SD card.

"Thank you so much. She will be so excited." Sarah said as she made her way to the truck.

When they got to Sarah's truck, Freddy turned to his sister. "Thanks for taking me. I hope you'll take me again?"

Sarah smiled at her younger brother. "Yeah, okay, I guess you behaved."

* * *

It was another week and no signs of Bob Kravis. The search had been scaled back the last few days. Cal was driving through Gold Canyon when the emergency text came. Climbers in distress at Miners Needle.

Cal replied he was nearby as he made his way up Peralta Road. He figured once he made it to the primitive road, he would cut through Quarter Circle U Ranch taking the road to the end and turning northward to Miner Needle.

Along the way, he had ascertained it was two climbers. One had fallen on the other and their lines were intertwined. The other climber was able to call on his cell phone, but they were both hanging about 25 feet from the top.

Cal knew he could maneuver his truck through the terrain close to Miners Needle. As he approached, he could see the two. Then he checked in one more time on the radio to see if there was any additional information. He got out his climbing equipment from the back of the truck and sprinted to the face of the needle.

Cal quickly set his line and started climbing up to the two as they dangled along the cliff.

"Can you hear me?" Cal yelled up. He yelled a few times until he got a response.

"Yes, I can hear you," came a voice.

"I'm Deputy Ligai. Are you hurt?"

"I think my one arm is broken and my friend seems a bit out of it. He's awake but just staring at me," the voice continued.

Cal yelled back up. "He might be in shock. I'm going to call in a helicopter and we'll get you both out of here."

Cal quickly radioed in the situation, and he would need air support. Cal methodologically made his way up to the climbers, sizing up the situation. He wondered if the climber had a concussion as he approached and was already thinking about getting him into a soft, portable stretcher to be hoisted by the helicopter.

Depending on the severity of the injuries to the second climber, he would need air support or slowly bring him down himself.

Cal started the trek to the two tangled climbers. As he got closer, he could hear the helicopter approaching. He radioed the copter that once he reached the climbers send down a portable stretcher and he would get the first climber inside.

"Cal, I'm about twenty minutes away." Came a voice over the radio. "It's Waylen Cambrai."

Cal apprised Waylen of the situation and said that the first climber may need to be transported to the ground as they came back for the second climber. His assistance on the ground would be needed.

Cal reached the two climbers. The one seemed in a fog with just a blank stare. Cal looked into the eyes of the second climber, who looked scared.

"Don't worry. We'll get you and your friend out of here. What's your name?"

"Jonathan, my name is Jonathan," the climber responded.

"Jonathan. You probably saved your friend's life. I'm going to maneuver an inflatable stretcher around him. We're going to be moving around. I need you to stay calm. For now, I'm securing your line. You are going to be fine," Cal reassured him.

The helicopter was above Cal and the climbers, sending down an inflatable stretcher. Cal reached for it and secured it to the line. The stretcher could be broken down to secure the injured party. Cal quickly secured the climbers next and placed an inflatable piece around each arm. This was then followed by inflatable pieces around each leg. Cal still needed to maneuver the main board behind him.

"Okay, Jonathan. How are you doing?" Cal asked.

"I'm fine. My right shoulder is in a lot of pain and my arm is getting numb." Jonathan replied.

"Just another minute. Once your friend is lifted by the helicopter, it should relieve some of the stress," Cal said as he slid the portable board under the climber. He attached all the pieces and made sure the line was secure to the helicopter before giving the thumbs up.

Cal looked below and he could see Waylen was down at the base of the needle. Cal looked at Jonathan and could tell he had nothing left and it would be best to have the copter drop them at the base of the needle.

"Rescue one, I'm going to ask you to quickly land the patient down to the base. We'll have someone quickly check vitals. In the meantime, hook a rope to the climber I have up here. Then switch them at the base. You take the first climber to the hospital, and I'll drive the second climber in my truck." Cal said over the radio.

The copter quickly had the climber on the stretcher on the ground and going up for the second one. Cal secured the second climber in a seat and quickly the copter took him down to the base. Cal quickly repelled to the bottom to meet Jonathon and Waylen.

As Cal met up with Waylen, the first climber on the stretcher was in the helicopter and taking off to a local hospital. Waylen was placing an inflatable cast on the climber's arm.

Waylen looked up at Cal. "Impressive job," He turned down to the climber, "Looks like a broken arm and some bruises and contusions. I have to say you were impressive, too!"

The climber smiled. "As long as he is okay, I'm good."

"As I said up there, you probably saved your friend's life," Cal turned to Waylen. "Let's get him in my truck. I can take him to the hospital in Mesa."

The two lifted their heads as they heard a vehicle head their way. Waylen quickly could tell it was a Tonto Forest pickup. "Cal looks like your friend is a little late. Good thing I was here." Waylen snickered.

"Waylen, I'm not sure what your issue is with Lil, but I hope you can get over it. You're probably two of the best people in these mountains." Cal replied.

"Maybe, but I don't trust her. Just remember I told you so," Waylen said as he helped the climber into the truck.

Lil's truck came to a stop as she got out and walked up to the two. "Looks like you have everything under control?"

Cal smiled at Lil. "Yes, between Waylen and the helicopter team, we are set."

Waylen made his way back to his vehicle. "Yep, we didn't need you this time, princess. This man is quite the expert climber."

Lil turned back to Cal. "Are you good?" She asked.

"Yes, I'm fine. I'm taking him," Cal said, nodding to the climber, "To one of the hospitals in Mesa. Talk to you later."

Lil smiled at Cal and then turned to her truck.

6

Although Jacob Waltz is most well known for finding the mine in the 1870s, he originally had a partner, Jacob Weiser. They had claimed to have found the Peralta mine, the "Lost Mine". It was believed the two worked the mine and then hid numerous caches of gold in the Superstition Mountains.

As time went on, they supposedly found more and more gold. Mysteriously, Jacob Weiser disappeared, never to be found. Jacob Waltz claimed that Weiser was attacked and killed by Apache Indians. While others claim Waltz killed him, claiming all the gold for himself.[1]

* * *

Cal was at his desk, tidying up all the loose ends. He couldn't help but think that it was weeks and no trace of Bob Kravis. The fliers remained out on social media, government buildings, and bulletin boards at most of the trailheads. Cal had checked in on the Kravis family. The phone calls from someone claiming to be Cal had stopped after Cal had stopped at the house.

Cal picked up the last folder in his tray on the desk, "Michael Kowalski". At first, it didn't ring a bell until he opened it up. It was the hiker he had searched for ten years ago with Deputy Anderson. The search was cut short as Michael Kowalski turned up at home, 3474 Meadow Drive, Coolidge, Arizona. Jose had told him it was common that the family to call back, and the person was not lost at all.

Cal thought there must be a way to minimize this from happening. He realized it wasn't a simple solution, but probably community awareness and possibly a drop box of routes for solo hikers at the trailheads. Possibly working with the Tonto Forest Rangers. He would talk to Lil about the best way to approach her boss.

Cal glanced at the report, not sure what he was looking for. Just over two weeks ago, he was doing the same thing with Bob Kravis's folder. He felt the urge to dial the number in the report, but for what? The family was in Coolidge, at least ten years ago. He tossed the folder back on the tray on the desk and headed out to get some lunch.

* * *

Over the radio came an injured hiker near Flatiron. The hiker was a 48-year-old man who slipped near the top of the trail before turning south to the top of Flatiron.

Cal turned his truck around and headed to the Superstitions. He listened to the responses. Waylen Cambrai came in. He was making his way up the trail with additional volunteers. He knew Jose was helping some hikers on Picketpost Mountain.

From the call, it appeared that the hiker had contusions on his head but was conscious. Reports said the hiker had a compound fracture. Waylen's team would carry the hiker to the top of Flatiron, where a helicopter could easily land and pick up the hiker.

As Cal drove north on Route 60, he continued to monitor the situation. Everything seemed under control. The team of volunteers was at the trailhead already and a team of five with a stretcher up Siphon Draw.

Cal continued to drive through Gold Canyon as the view of the Superstitions overtook the horizon. Considering that Cal was in the Superstition Mountains hundreds of times he was always taken by its view, its danger, its mystery.

In another fifteen minutes, Cal was pulling into the State Park. He raced to the far parking lot closest to the Siphon Draw trailhead. As he got closer, he noticed the familiar vehicles, including two Tonto Forest pickups. Standing behind one of them were Lil and another ranger.

Cal parked his truck and headed over to Lil. "Lil, I didn't know you were here."

"I just got here," Lil continued as she turned to the other ranger, "Cal, I don't think you met Thurman Kelly, a new ranger for the Tonto Forest."

"I don't believe so," as Cal put his hand out.

"Pleasure to meet you, sir," the new ranger replied with a firm handshake.

Cal looked up as she could see the helicopter getting close to the top of Flatiron. The radio was lively as the pilot and Waylen communicated about picking up the injured hiker. The three in the parking lot listened to each word until the helicopter took off with the hiker.

Cal got on the radio. "Waylen, nice job. I'm down in the lot. I'll wait for you to get back."

The rough voice replied. "No need to hang around. We did a great job. We don't need a pat on the back."

Cal put his radio to the side and shook his head.

"Cal, Waylen has to be restrained," Lil continued. "He more or less told Thurman to stay here and wait for him in case anyone showed up and to let them know it was under control. Cal, he has no authority, and he knows that. He was taking advantage of Thurman being new."

"Lil, technically the sheriff and the volunteers are to handle this. You're unique in that you're both a Forest Ranger and a volunteer for SAR. Look, I admit Waylen can be rough, but he's good and committed to helping those in the mountains. The group thinks highly of him, so yes, he has to be harnessed in, but gently," Cal said, as he then turned to Thurman. "Thurman, let me show you what we record on the laptop for any rescue. It might be useful for you to see what we look for. I'll get any missing pieces from Waylen when he comes down."

Cal showed Thurman the report as Lil walked off to her truck and made a phone call. She continually scanned the path that Waylen and the other volunteers would come back on. Eventually, she heard Waylen's loud voice and within a few minutes, saw him on the horizon.

Lil heard a car approach and turned as if it was one of the local television news teams. She turned to Cal. "Cal, do you want to take care of this?"

Cal looked at the van and then turned to Lil, "No, Lil, can you handle it? I'll finish up with Thurman."

Lil wasn't too happy about talking to the reporter, especially since Cal was here. She walked up to the van as the reporter quickly started asking Lil for information. Lil debriefed them on the situation.

"Are they coming back this way?" the reporter asked Lil.

"The hiker was taken in a helicopter. If you want to take a few seconds of the Flatiron in the sunset for the news, that might be an excellent shot."

The cameraman took a few different angles of Flatiron from the parking lot and then the team packed up and left. As the van turned down and then out of the parking lot, Waylen and his team arrived and turned to Cal, then nodded to the news van.

"Is our little girl and the Tonto Forest team trying to take the credit?"

Cal walked close to Waylen and spoke so that no one could make out his words but Waylen. "I told her to take care of them when they pulled in. I'm not sure what your issue is with her, but I can't have it. You're not this way with anyone else."

Lil had seen them speaking and walked up to the two. "Good evening, Waylen. Nice job up there."

"I'm sure that's what you told the news. Taking the credit, I'm sure." Waylen snickered.

"Waylen, you are an asshole," Lil replied as she turned to her truck.

Within ten minutes, everyone was packed up and on their way.

* * *

A few days later, Cal was headed home from training some volunteers with Jose rappelling at Picacho State Park. He needed to get back to the office in Florence to fill out a few reports. He headed down Route 287 into Coolidge.

As he entered the town, he could see the lane closure for some of the road construction. He wasn't in the mood to sit in traffic. He would rather be moving, even if it didn't save time. After a few minutes in the traffic, he turned right, up one of the local streets. He knew any of the streets would get him to Attaway Road where he could get to Florence from there. Although as he looked down the street he was on, it appeared to be a dead end. He turned left again, looking for a cross street to get him out of town.

He stopped at the stop sign, trying to decide if he should go straight for a few more blocks or turn right. He looked at the street sign, Butte Road & Meadow Drive. It sounded familiar but still wasn't sure, so he turned right on Meadow Drive. He didn't go more than a few hundred feet, and it hit Cal. Meadow Drive, he pulled his pickup to the side of the road. He turned on the computer in his truck and typed in Michael Kowalski.

There it was, 3474 Meadow Drive. Cal looked at the house numbers in front of him, as he was in the 2000s. He slowly drove up the street until he came to 3474. Cal looked at the home, deciding what, if anything, he should do. He felt drawn to speak with Michael about getting lost in the Superstitions and how could have been prevented. Damn, I'm here for a reason, he thought, as he placed the truck in park. He got out and walked up the broken cement walkway to the front door.

He knocked on the door and an old woman answered the door.

"Hello, is this the Kowalski residence?" Cal asked.

"Yes, it is," the old woman continued. "Is there something wrong? Is my husband okay?

"Oh yes, I think," Cal said, a bit off guard, "I'm here about Michael."

The woman dropped the glass she was holding. "They found him?"

"I'm here from the Pinal County Search and Rescue, Deputy Ligai. I was actually hoping to speak with him. Sounds like he left home?" Cal asked.

"Yes, ten years ago. He went hiking in the Superstitions and we never heard from him again," the old woman said.

"I remember that case. I thought he came home, and the search was called off." Cal said, trying to figure out where the confusion was. "I was hoping to speak with him about the time in the mountains."

The woman snapped back bewildered, "Like I said, he's been missing for ten years now. The sheriff's office would call every week for a few months with any updates, then it became monthly until they told us they thought he was sighted in Las Vegas."

"Who were you speaking with? Do you remember the officer?" Cal asked.

"It was so long ago. It was on the phone. There were multiple people. Mostly a man with a deep voice and sometimes a woman," she answered.

"I'm sorry, Ms. Kowalski, there must have been a mix-up in the notes. We'll fix it on our end. I apologize again," Cal said as he lifted his hat and headed back to his truck. Twice families called in and the hiker didn't show up. He wanted to get back to the office to see who followed up on this case. What was going on?

* * *

Cal went back to the office and got into the database. So how do I find out if there are any more cases like this? A missing hiker then the family calls in that they are home.

He picked up the file on Michael Kowalski, that was still on his desk. He wanted to check who spoke with the family and who filed the report. Deputy Johnson. He wasn't familiar with him, but he was sure Deputy Rodriguez would give him the skinny on Deputy Johnson.

He looked back up at the screen. He tried filtering a few different things, but nothing worked. The outcome wasn't specific enough. A few hundred reports a year, times ten years, or maybe even longer. He was becoming more frustrated than anything and he knew the people that could help him in the database wouldn't be back till the morning.

Okay. He knew there might be someone who might remember another case with similar outcomes. He pulled out his phone and dialed.

"Lil, it's me. Did you have dinner already?" Cal continued. "Oh, how about a drink? Sure, your place. Text me the address and I'll see you shortly."

Cal maneuvered his way through the neighborhoods of Apache Junction until his GPS had him pull down a small side street. He parked in front of the address Lil had given him. He saw the front door open and the light from inside which lit the small patio in the front. As Cal approached the front door, he saw Lil in the kitchen at the back of the small ranch.

"Well, come on in," she looked up as Cal stepped inside. "Bourbon?" She poured two drinks before Cal acknowledged.

"Yes, that would be great."

She handed him one glass.   "Let's sit in the back. It's a full moon and I have a magnificent view of the Supes. The two stepped onto the dark porch in the back and sat looking out at the Superstition Mountains.

"What a view," Cal said as he adjusted his seat.

"You picked a good night to come out here, full moon and it's hovering over the Supes," Lil turned to Cal. "Like it was waiting for you."

Cal took a sip of his drink.   "It always has a mysterious feel to it, doesn't it?"

"Since man has set on these mountains, it has always had mystical powers. Many people can sense it, some better than others," Lil said as she pointed out. "Looks like a few people are camping on top of the Flatiron."

Cal could set the glow of a fire on top of the mountain. "The way the lights moving I'm guessing some lanterns?" Cal said as he squinted at the mountain.

"Come here if you want a better look," Lil said as she stood and made her way to the other side of the patio.

As Cal followed her, he could see she had a telescope pointed at the mountain.

"Cal, give me a second," as she adjusted the telescope.   "Yeah, looks like at least a half dozen up there. Some with head lanterns," as she stepped aside for Cal to look.

"This is very clear. Impressive," Cal said as he watched the campers walking on top of Flatiron.

"So what's going on, Cal? What can I help you with?" Lil smiled.

"Do I only reach out when I need something? I'll need to put an end to that," Cal responded.

"It's okay. I don't mind being your go-to gal," Lil smiled then looked at Cal not knowing how he might respond, "I mean go-to person."

"I think they both sound good to me," Cal continued. "It's about Bob Kravis and Michael Kowalski."

"Bob Kravis, okay, he is the young man missing that you spoke to his father. Who is Michael Kowalski?" Lil asked.

"Do you remember about ten years back when we both were searching the Supes and there we also got a call that the lost hiker went back home," Cal explained.

"Okay, that's who you were referring to before?" Lil said.

"Right. The thing is, I spoke with Michael Kowalski's mother today. He never returned home either."

Lil looked at Cal in disbelief. "What. That's crazy. Are you sure?" Lil stopped herself. "I mean, I know you're sure. I just can't believe it."

"You said there were others who the search was called off as the family called that they were back home. Do you remember any specifics on the others? Dates, names, anything," Cal asked.

"Oh wow, let me think," Lil paused. "I'm sure there are a few. Can you let me check my records at the office tomorrow? I'll text you anything I come up with."

"Even if it's a few, I'd appreciate it. Then it's like who is doing this and why," Cal asked.

"There has to be an explanation," Lil said as she stood to take Cal's empty glass. "Anything new from the Kravis kid," Lil asked as she walked into the kitchen to pour them another drink.

"No, nothing new. I was almost hoping it was a mean neighbor who was vindictive but with the same thing as Michael Kowalski. I mean, what could it be, someone who is listening on shortwave radio?" Cal said.

"You know, you might be on to something. Maybe a sick mind," Lil said.

"Or someone who lost a loved one in the mountains and now wants others to see the same fate. So anything you find might help," Cal said as he took the glass from Lil.

The two sat in the yard, trying to figure out who would do something like Cal had presented to her.

"I'm guessing we will have to keep looking for clues," Cal said as he took a sip of his drink and sat back in his chair, looking up at the moon. "Lil, this view is incredible."

"Yeah, I like it. I used to live in an apartment in Mesa when I first became a Ranger for the Tonto Forest. I always kept my eyes open for something available closer to the mountains. And one day I was driving down the street and here it was. It needs some updates, but I live a pretty simple life," Lil replied.

"How long have you been a ranger in the Tonto Forest?" Cal inquired.

"Over fifteen years. They've asked me to transfer a few times. Thankfully, the sheriff's department has always stepped in on my behalf that I'm needed for the rescues because of my knowledge of the mountains," Lil continued as she stood up. "Cal, I'll be counting on you if it happens again."

Cal took the last sip of his drink and stood up. "Lil, you can count on me."

The two looked into each other's eyes in the moonlight. Both seemed to be at a loss for words. Lil reached out her hand to take Cal's empty glass.

"I'd pour you another drink, but I'm not sure what would happen," Lil smiled. "So we'll keep it at two drinks, at least for tonight."

Cal looked into her eyes and smiled. "One of us has to have some control."

"Don't always count on me," Lil said as the two continued back into the house.

Cal chuckled. "Sounds like we might get in trouble down the road."

"Maybe, maybe not," Lil smiled back as she walked Cal to the front door. "Cal, I'll look through my notes in the morning and see if I can remember any other cases where the family called us back that the hiker came back home."

"Thank you, Lil, Thank you for everything. For this evening, and well, even before tonight," Cal said as he leaned over and gave her a hug and a peck on the cheek.

"Cal, you're a good guy. We'll figure all this out. The universe has a plan for us," Lil replied, as she stood in the doorway, Cal made his way to his car.

Cal got in his vehicle and watched as Lil waved and turned back into her house and he saw the lights one by one turn off. As he turned the ignition of the car, he thought to himself, he was not looking for this, but it sure felt good.

7

Elisha Marcus Reavis was a hermit of the Superstitions and established his homestead in the Superstitions in the late 1870s. He was known for his fruits and vegetables and would travel to nearby towns to sell them. He was somewhat of a local legend, as tales of his run-ins with the Apache Indians were well known. In the Spring of 1896, after not being seen for some time, a prospector went looking for him and found him dead.[1]

* * *

The next morning Cal got to the office and with the help of Betty, came up through multiple sources, three other instances where a family member called in the missing hiker as returned.

Lil had sent over names and dates that she found. Four names and then an additional date. Cal smirked. Lil did a better job at recording some of this.

Cal pulled all the files with names and by cross-referencing the date, found a fifth instance. What did they have in common, if anything, three males and two females? Ages ranged from 19 to 47 and they lived in four different towns.

Next, he pulled their names to see if any had any type of record. Trish Stevens had a speeding ticket two years ago, but the other four had nothing. He took the remaining names to Betty.

"Can you find out if any of these people voted, let's say," as Cal looked at the dates of the incidents, "In the last four years."

"Sure, give me a little time. I'll find out the last time they voted for all of them. That's if they voted." Betty replied.

Cal sat back at his desk, toggling from one file to the other. Was he missing anything? Maybe all these people made it back home. He needed to be patient to see if there were others.

Betty finally came back with a folder. "Cal, two of them voted within the last two years, and I took the liberty to look up the other two names and found one moved to Michigan. I had a phone number, so I called. Seemed like the real deal."

"And the last one?" Cal asked.

"Nothing, Linda Sharper," Betty replied.

Cal knew that was the one who Lil had a date for, but no name. "Thanks, Betty. If you think of any other sort we might do, maybe we are missing someone."

Cal looked at the folder Betty had given him on Linda Sharper. The husband called in three years ago. Thirty-one and lived in Superior, Arizona. With two phone numbers, Cal figured he had nothing to lose.

The first number went right to voicemail, with no name on the message. He dialed the second number and a male voice answered.

"Hello, this is Deputy Ligai from Pinal County's Search and Rescue. I'm calling regarding Linda Sharper," Cal said.

There was a long pause before he heard a reply. "I've been dreading this call. You found her remains?"

"No, I'm afraid not. I just wanted to check a few things on file and if you could confirm them, it would be most helpful," Cal answered.

"Sure go ahead. It's been three years. I'll answer the best I remember," came the voice.

"It looks like it was the first of February that you called in that your wife didn't return on a hike in the Superstitions. Is that correct?" Cal asked.

"Yes. I wanted to wait because she would get caught up with photos and getting some pictures of sunrises and sunsets. So the night after, she never came home, so that's when I called your office."

"And after that, what happened?" Cal asked.

"Well, nothing. Your office called that she was still missing and that you would continue to search. The one deputy stopped over a few times over the next month, and he called me weekly," the man said as his voice cracked.

"Do you remember the deputy's name, by any chance?"

"A few people called and the deputy stopped over. I don't remember his name. I'm sure you have that, anyway."

"We do. Just wanted to speak with you with a new set of eyes and ears." Cal continued. "If we get any new information, we'll call you immediately."

"Thank you." Came the voice from the phone as he hung up.

A third time, something wasn't right. He placed Linda Sharper's file next to Michael Kowalski's. There it was something in common. The same deputy followed up with the family, Deputy Johnson.

Cal walked over to Betty. "Deputy Johnson, I don't think I've met him. Do you have his phone number?"

Betty looked up at Cal. "Bucky Johnson was killed last year on a call. There was a domestic disturbance, and he was shot. He died the next day."

"Bucky, yeah, I remember that," Cal answered as he turned back to his desk. He wasn't sure he had any answers. He wasn't even sure he had the right questions.

Over the next few days, Cal reached out to all the names on the list just to be sure the information was accurate. He had a lengthy conversation with the sheriff who, collectively, decided to continue to look into these cases but didn't want it advertised on what he was working on, at least until he had some concrete facts.

* * *

So after some persuasion, Freddy got his sister Sarah to agree to a longer more challenging hike in the Superstitions. He had talked into driving out to Canyon Lake and heading down Boulder Canyon. They had got to Canyon Lake marina early, as they had heard there were only a few parking spots designated for the hikers.

They crossed Route 88 and started up the first hill. As they moved up the hill, they got a great view of the canyon and La Barge Creek below. Freddy was keeping track of how far they had traveled on his phone. They stopped for a drink of water and Freddy saw they had only hiked a half mile, but it seemed farther.

They both drank and started back up the hill. "Sarah, I heard once we get up this hill it's an incredible view," Freddy said as he was wondering if his sister was enjoying the trail.

"That's what I heard. The first mile is a bear, but after that, the views are awesome," Sarah replied.

Sure enough, when they got to the top of the hill, the view of Battleship Mountain and Weavers Needle in the background was breathtaking.

Battleship Mountain stood alone with the creek rolling to the east side of it. Weavers Needle was one of the most notable places in the Superstitions, which was named after Pauline Weaver, one of the first scouts to cover the Superstitions.

"Wow," Freddy said as he stood atop the hill.

"Remember, we said we'll go out 2 1/2 miles and then return. Everyone told us that's a good distance for the first time on this trail," Sarah said as she placed her water bottle in her backpack.

"Well 1.1 miles down. Looks easier from this point. Maybe we can go farther," Freddy questioned his sister.

"Don't make me regret this. We said 2 1/2 miles out. We're covering a bit of elevation," she snapped back at her brother.

They continued down the trail. With each twist, Battleship Mountain and Weavers Needle became more pronounced on the horizon. They could move quicker, as the terrain was easier to navigate. Freddy continued to monitor the distance on his phone, although he didn't want to let his sister know, at least until she asked, as he was hoping to go farther.

They finally came to a ledge where other hikers had stopped to hydrate and have some snacks. The colors of the mountains with the dark green vegetation were breathtaking.

"I guess this is the place, the 2 1/2-mile point," Sarah asked.

"Yeah, it is," Freddy replied disappointingly.

"So how are you feeling? Want to go out another half mile, down to the creek below," Sarah said, pointing to the trail headed to the creek.

"Hell yeah," he replied.

The two headed down and it was easiest enough as they were walking down a decline. Sarah was hoping it wasn't a mistake. Just before reaching the creek, the path crossed an area with thick vegetation. Freddy stopped to get a quick drink there, as it was one of the few areas that had some shade. As he drank, he thought he saw someone in the bushed to the side. He placed the cap down and took a step into the bushes.

"Hello," Freddy called out.

Sarah looked at him. "What are you doing? Who are you talking to?"

"I thought I saw someone. I guess not. Maybe it was a bird," he laughed.

The two continued down to the creek and they looked up at Battleship Mountain. It looked so large as they stood in front of it. Sarah turned back to where they had come from.

"Now we have to hike back up that, well in a bit," she said, as she enjoyed the view as well.

Eventually, the two made their way back to the trail they had taken to the creek. The first half mile was almost all incline to where they had stopped before. After they rested there, they continued back along the winding trail.

A few times Freddy scanned the rocks and vegetation as if were looking for something.

"Keep your eyes on the trail Freddy, or you're going to slip," Sarah said, watching her brother in front of her.

"I know, but," Freddy paused, "I feel like someone is watching us."

"Sounds like you might need more water," she laughed at her brother.

They continued back to the trailhead. The entire way Freddy had an airy feeling.

* * *

By now, Cal knew most of the deputies' and Tonto Forest Rangers' schedules. Things were always changing and if an emergency came up, he would be the first to know. He knew on Friday mornings Lil would be at the First Water Trailhead assisting hikers with any questions or concerns.

As he pulled into the dirt parking lot, he could see Lil by the map pointing out something to a group of hikers. He couldn't help but smile as Lil's excitement about these mountains was contagious. She was a wealth of knowledge to the hikers, as well as to him.

As the hikers stepped away, Cal walked up to Lil. "Good morning, Lil."

"Good morning, Deputy," Lil replied with a smile. "What brings you out here? Come looking for gold?"

"No calls in a few days, but the weekend is here." Cal turned to the full parking lot. "Let's hope no one needs us."

"You never know. I had a group of four this morning heading down the Dutchman's trail to Red Tanks Trail, eventually to Woodbury. They have enough provisions for two nights. Another couple headed to Battleship Mountain, eventually to Calvary trail circling back to the Dutchman by late tomorrow. They seemed prepared as well." Lil said, checking her notes.

"I wish we could clone you and have you at every trailhead," Cal smirked.

"You know as well as I do, the best way to prevent an accident. And, I like to know all the hikers are safe. I like to know where they are headed and when I'll expect them back," Lil said as she jotted down a few items in her notebook. "Cal, did you find anything about those two cases?"

"I found a third, Linda Sharper. She and the other two were the only ones I found that were actually still missing even though someone called in and claimed they had returned home. Frankly, I don't see anything to link them. The only thing I can tell is someone went to a lot of effort to cover this up. The sheriff and I have spoken with a lot of people and nothing makes sense."

"What are you going to do? Anyone remember names, faces, anything?" Lil asked.

"No. The sheriff's department checked in on the family. We even had an EMT with the Kowalski family afterward. But whoever they looked at, it wasn't Michael Kowalski."

"There has to be a logical explanation. Mixed up paperwork, something." Lil replied.

"It's on my mind constantly," Cal said as a group of hikers were gathering in their cars. "That's when we're not rescuing someone."

Lil turned as she saw the hikers approaching, then back to Cal. "Let's have dinner tonight, no interruptions."

"Okay. I'll pick you up at six," Cal said with a big grin.

"Perfect. I'll figure out where you just bring your wallet," Lil said as she then turned to the hikers who had made their way to the trailhead entrance. "Good morning. Where are you folks headed out this morning?"

* * *

That evening, Cal picked up Lil, and they went to a small tavern on the Apache Trail in the town of Apache Junction. They walked and parked themselves at a pub table in front of the bar as a waitress came up to the table with menus and promptly took a drink order.

"Cal, besides good company, a good meal, and drinks, our goal should be to behave." Lil laughed.

"So what I hear you saying," Cal smiled as he looked into Lil's eyes, "Our goals are a little different."

From that point on, the two bantered and laughed for the next few hours. The waitress came by and asked if they wanted another drink. The two looked at each other as Lil turned her gaze away from Cal. He responded to the waitress without taking his eyes off Lil, "I think we are good. I have to get this lady home."

Cal pulled into Lil's driveway and placed his car in park. He looked at Lil and for the first time, neither one could think of something to talk about. Cal leaned forward and kissed her.

Her lips moved in perfect unison with his, and when he backed off for a moment, he could still feel her lips on his. Lil pulled him back in for another kiss.

When she stopped to catch her breath, she looked into Cal's eyes, that twinkled in the moonlight.

"So what you're saying, Cal, is we actually have the same goal?" Lil continued. "You are coming in', as her eyes hypnotized Cal.

The two walked in the door as Lil turned on the front hallway light. She tossed her keys on the table and then turned to Cal. The two were embraced as Cal looked into Lil's eyes as he kissed her. They maneuvered their way into the living room without separating and both fell on the couch.

"So I guess we aren't going to talk about work," Lil laughed.

"I sure hope not," Cal responded as he moved Lil's hair back and kissed her neck.

"Cal let's move into the next room. It will be more comfortable," Lil said as she stood from the couch and took Cal's hand, and led him into the bedroom.

Cal woke up a few hours later. He heard a faint crackling noise. At first, not remembering where he was. Cal turned his head on the pillow and saw Lil asleep. He quietly got out of bed as he tried to remember where the bathroom was. He then made his way into the kitchen and opened the cupboard to get a glass. If he didn't have a few glasses of water, he was going to feel the drinks tomorrow.

As he was finishing the glass of water, he still was hearing a crackling noise, louder. He quietly made his way through the house and found it was just the shortwave radio that was on. He turned it off and headed back to the kitchen.

He could see the Superstition Mountains perfectly through the window above the sink. Was it his imagination, as he thought he saw a flickering light in the mountains?

He focused and could tell the light was man-made and was not moving. It almost seemed like a code. Cal focused on it and quickly could tell it wasn't Morse code. He opened the door to the backyard and continued to watch the light. It appeared to be a series of lights at different intervals and stopped twice to repeat. Then eventually it was gone.

Maybe he was imagining it. He went back into the kitchen for another glass of water and then made his way into the dark bedroom. Cal was trying to find his clothes with only the moonlight that came through the window. He eventually found them all and dressed, hoping not to disturb Lil.

Cal reached down to kiss Lil on her forehead. "Are you leaving?" Lil said as she opened her eyes.

"Yes, we both have a full day tomorrow," Cal said, looking down at Lil.

"You know my schedule already, don't you?" Lil smiled back at Cal.

"It's my job too, yours and everyone on our team." Cal turned as he made his way out of the home.

8

In June 1931, Adolph Ruth went into the Superstition Mountains, with what he believed to be maps of the lost treasure in the Superstitions. A week later, an extensive search was underway as he never returned to camp. It wasn't until six months later Adolph Ruth's skull was found near the Dutchman's Trail and Bull Pass Trail, with evidence that suggests he was shot in the head. It was another month till his body was found near the east slope of Black Top Mesa, almost a mile from where they had found his skull.[1]

* * *

Sarah and Freddy had gotten into a routine of weekend hikes. For Sarah, it was easier for her to go with her brother than to ask one of her girlfriends who needed to make a big plan in the morning. For Freddy, it was the only way he could go on one, as the Superstition

Mountains were too far to ride on his bike with any of his friends. He could also suggest some trails that were farther out. Ones that his parents or his friends' parents wouldn't approve of.

Today the two of them agreed on the Broadway Cave. Not as long of a hike, but the large rocks that covered the trail made it slower than other trails. They headed up the Monument Canyon Trail and first checked out the remains of a fireplace chimney. Then it was to the cave. The last 100 yards were a challenging scramble, but they had minor difficulty as they made it up.

The cave itself did not go far back, but more of an alcove. Remains of a campfire and some graffiti were at the far end of the cave. They both stopped and looked out over where they had started from and looked down at the town of Apache Junction.

"This was short, kind of too easy for us, Sarah," Freddy chuckled as he continued. "Maybe on the way back, we can do a bit of Jacobs Crosscut. Just a bit, then come back."

Sarah looked at her brother, "Well, just a mile or so, then we turn around. But I tell you what, let's plan a long hike next week."

Sarah started heading down and Freddy was to follow. But something caught his eye on the other side of the cave. Freddy made his way to the other side of the cave but was not sure anymore what he saw a second ago. Then he heard some rocks falling to the side of the cave. Was it Sarah? Did she take another way down? He ran to the edge and saw nothing. He looked to his left, and he saw his sister taking the same path they had taken down the mountain.

As he made his way to catch up to Sarah, he heard rocks rolling again. He turned and saw a young person running down the mountain. The person turned and looked up at Freddy. Their eyes met and Freddy could have sworn it was the same clothes but a larger person from a few weeks back.

Freddy yelled down to the person, "Hello?"

Sarah then turned and realized her brother wasn't behind her and was still back up near the cave.

"Let's go, Freddy. If you want to do a long hike next week, this isn't helping," Sarah yelled up to him.

Freddy turned from his sister back to where he saw the person who was now gone. He figured it wasn't worth bringing up this to his sister, so he quickly caught up to her and they completed an additional mile on Jacobs Crosscut as Sarah had promised. Freddy continued to survey the desert to see if the person was going to show up again.

*   *   *

With the increase of Search and Rescue operations in the Superstitions, Pinal County finally received funds for an additional helicopter. They had purchased a UH -60 Black Hawk.

This helicopter, introduced in the late 1970s, could carry up to 15 people, was extremely versatile, and was outfitted with numerous devices that can be used in a variety of ways. Its low maintenance helped in its selection, but with such a large price tag, it was planned to be utilized for other state and federal needs.

The sheriff met Cal at the Mesa Gateway Airport for the arrival of the helicopter, already named Aurora 5. Austin Johnson was the senior pilot for the County and was one of two pilots who were selected to fly a majority of the Aurora 5 flights. The three men stood on the airfield as Aurora 5 landed.

The sheriff turned to the other two, proud that they had been able to secure funds for the helicopter. "She is a beauty. Love the Arizona flag so prominent on its side."

"Sir, she sure is. Sheriff, I don't know how you did it, but happy to fly her," Johnson said, not taking his eyes off the helicopter.

"We'll be doing some border patrol work with this as well. Anywhere we can help out. Bring back some of that money," the sheriff replied.

Cal knew the statistics. More people were visiting the Superstitions, more hikers, and more rescues. Cal turned to Austin. "I'm sure you're going to be quite busy and be enjoying it."

The three of them laughed as the pilot who had flown the helicopter made his way over to the trio and introduced himself.

"Gentlemen, Stan Borbachek," as he handed over the paperwork to Austin. "She is all yours. An interesting bird. Of course, not any weapons as many have, but the night vision and surveillance on this baby are second to none. You'll be able to see a scorpion crawling through the night."

"I think we'll be busy enough not to worry about the scorpions," Cal replied.

The three walked over to the helicopter. Austin immediately sat in the cockpit. The sheriff went into the back of the copter. He was impressed by how spacious it was. Being able to carry an additional dozen people, he knew he was going to keep this bird busy.

Cal walked around the outside. It was larger than most of the Search & Rescue helicopters the county and state had. He looked under the helicopter and could see all the equipment and options this helicopter had.

He knew not only for helping in the Superstition Mountains but across the state, this helicopter was going to save lives.

* * *

Cal knew it probably didn't look good to others that he was spending so much time with Lil. It had started out as work, as she was probably the most knowledgeable of the mountain trails and landscape, but they had formed a bond.

Some drinks lead to dinner once a week, then a few times a week to where Cal was spending nights at Lil's house. He wasn't a direct supervisor, so there was no issue, but he still wanted to keep it quiet, although he had no intentions of sneaking around. If it came out, it came out.

Cal pulled into Lil's driveway and walked up to the front door. Before he could knock, the door swung open, and Lil greeted him with a big smile.

"Are you ready to go?" Cal asked.

"Do you mind if we stay in tonight? I wouldn't mind a quiet evening." Lil said as she placed her arms around Cal's neck.

"When you ask me that way, I think we know the answer." Cal chuckled.

"Good, because I've already been cooking. Have you ever had Apache stew or Apache fry bread," Lil said as she took Cal by the hand into the kitchen.

Cal could smell the aroma of the stew cooking. "No, what's in Apache stew?"

"It's venison roast, bell peppers, hominy, some endive," Lil continued as she stirred the pot, "Potatoes, carrots, spices. I think you'll like it."

"Well, I don't think I've had it. It sure smells good." Cal replied.

Lil went to the fridge and pulled out a beer and handed it to Cal. "This will have to hold you over."

The two enjoyed their evening as they ate, laughed, and spoke of the mysterious mountain on the horizon. Eventually, they made their way to Lil's bedroom and they held each other tightly till they fell asleep.

Cal woke up and grabbed a beer from the refrigerator and sat on the back patio. It was a full moon, and the Superstitions looked even more mysterious tonight. It looked like active campers up there as he periodically saw flashes of lights coming from the mountains.

Cal looked at the moonlight as it hit the sporadic clouds, which took on the glow of the moon. He could hear a few coyotes in the distance howling at the moon. Cal turned his focus back on the silhouette of the Superstitions.

It seemed to Cal that the blinking lights almost had a pattern. He took another sip of beer and continued to watch. Sure enough, within a few minutes, it repeated. Cal went into the kitchen and opened the drawers until he found a pen and some paper.

He went outside and jotted down how long each burst of light was. They seemed to range from 1 to 3 seconds. He recorded the numbers until the lights stopped for a minute and then it started again. Sure enough, within a few minutes, the signal repeated several times. 2 - 2 - 1 - 3 - 2 - 1 - 1 - 3 - 3.

What did it mean? He stopped writing the numbers down, but the light kept going. He heard Lil in the kitchen as he placed the paper in his pocket.

"I was wondering where you went," Lil said as she stepped out onto the patio and put her arm around Cal's waist.

"I hope I didn't wake you. I couldn't sleep, so I figured I'd enjoy the scenery of your yard as I listen to coyotes." Cal responded.

Lil took the beer out of Cal's hand and took a sip. "Are you coming back to bed or spending more time with the coyotes?" Lil asked.

"I'm coming in." Cal continued, "It's those lights. There is a pattern."

"It's your imagination. I see lights almost every night."

"Watch. Two seconds, two seconds, one second." Cal turned to Lil. "It goes on for a few more minutes than repeats."

"Well, it must be kids playing games," Lil said as she took Cal by the hand back into the house, back into the bedroom.

* * *

Cal sat at his desk, looking at his computer. Still nothing on Bob Kravis. The local search and rescue volunteers were out for weeks looking for him. They had sent emails with areas they had hiked and searched.

Cal had added an old picture of Michael Kowalski with a description of what he was wearing to the list of missing people. The same for Linda Sharper. It still bothered Cal that there may be others out there missing that he was unaware of.

Cal had spent a fair amount of his free time hiking in the Superstitions, hoping to find anything on Bob Kravis. Maybe some clues about Michael Kowalski and Linda Sharper. It still bothered him that someone had called the families impersonating officers for the Pinal Sheriff's office. So in his mind, it was more than someone lost in the Superstitions, there was more to it.

Were there more than those three that they should be looking for? Lil had shared some information she kept, but nothing jumped out. Cal had spent time with so many of the volunteers over the last few weeks, especially those who have been volunteering for years. No one remembered any other situations similar to that or Kravis, Kowalski, and Sharper.

It was time to have a long conversation with Waylen. On one hand, he didn't want to stir the pot with him. On the other, Waylen had been around for a long time and knew what he was talking about. Cal took another hike to the Massacre Grounds, and if Waylen was free, it would be a good idea to hear what he had to say about the two missing hikers.

Cal pulled onto the road to First Water Trailhead. He headed down the dirt road to the parking lot for the Massacre Grounds and he saw Waylen was already there.

Cal pulled up to Waylen's truck and got out. "Waylen, thanks for meeting me. It's still bothering me that there has been no trace of Bob Kravis."

"We get a few of those now and then. This mountain has lost a lot of people," Waylen continued as the two started up the trailhead. "With the temperatures climbing we're going to have more hikers in trouble because of not bringing enough water. I wonder if we could post something at the Trailheads on the amount of water to bring."

"That's a great idea. I'm sure the Tonto Forest could post something at each trailhead." Cal answered.

"So I take it no leads with Bob Kravis seen somewhere else, maybe a runaway," Waylen asked.

"No, nothing. You said you get these now and then. How many have you seen like that? The family calls back that the person is home." Cal asked.

"I would guess one every year or two. You could probably look up some of that information. I'm sure the sheriff's office has all that." Waylen replied.

"It's a little tough to sort from the database, but I've found a handful. The Tonto Rangers had some data as well." Cal said as he kept an eye along the path, hoping to find something on Bob Kravis.

"You mean Lil. She seems to take a lot of notes." Waylen interjected.

"I remember when I first joined the sheriff's department, the same thing happened with Michael Kowalski. Do you remember that?" Cal asked.

"Oh yeah, I remember that one. There were a few others that stand out," Waylen continued. "The one that stands out to me most is the one that makes me have a funny feeling about your girl."

Cal knew he was speaking of Lil when he mentioned your girl. "What one is that Waylen?"

"Sandy Davenport. It was about a year before the Kowalski hiker. A woman in her early 30s goes hiking on the Reavis Ranch Trail. We had a large group of volunteers and Lil ends up sending most of them down either the Reavis Gap, Fire Line Trail, or the Two Bar Ridge Trail. She says she and the other rangers had Reavis Ranch Trail covered. Turns out only a few rangers were helping her. I blame your predecessor for letting her take the lead. Anyway, the family called the next morning that she was home. It turned out fine, but when I'd spoken to the other rangers, they weren't on the Reavis Trail with her. I just got a bad feeling about her from that day."

"I don't think I heard anything about Sandy Davenport," Cal said as he quickly thought of what he found in the Sheriff's computer and what Lil told him about.

"There are a few others, just don't have them at the top of my head," Waylen said as he stopped to take a drink of water.

"So here we are, looking for Bob Kravis. Maybe he is in these mountains, maybe he ran away. We just don't know," Cal continued. "So I reached out to the Kowalski family, and they were a bit confused as their son Michael never came home."

Waylen stopped in his tracks. "Are you telling me the same thing that happened to Bob Kravis and it took ten years for someone to find out?

"The sheriff's department has him as a missing person with a new photo of how he might look today," Cal said.

"So, on the assumption he is living somewhere else. We know if he is found in the mountains, it will just be a pile of bones." Waylen snickered.

"I'm afraid you're correct. That's why we didn't say a missing hiker in the Superstitions. Our hope is he is somewhere else. Somewhere healthy and alive."

Cal thought about telling Waylen more, including how someone was calling the Kravis family, claiming to be the sheriff's department. Cal wasn't sure what that would lead to and if Waylen could hold his tongue on that. The two continued to search along the Massacre Grounds Trail. Twice Cal came across the primitive drawing of a group of warriors or hunters with a large white warrior looking down and the group below.

"So many drawings in these mountains," Waylen said.

"Yes. This particular one seems to pop up lately," Cal answered.

Waylen looked at the drawing. "Yeah, I've seen this in a few places."

Cal shared with Waylen about the new Search and Rescue helicopter arriving. Waylen was just as excited as the others. He had to give Waylen a lot of credit, as he was very dedicated to finding lost and injured people in the Superstition Mountains.

Waylen knew the Superstitions inside and out. Only one person knew them better, Lil.

9

In 1892, a barefoot young thirteen-year-old boy, Charlie Dobbie, was found shot in the back with his head smashed by a large rock at JF Ranch. The ranch had been ransacked, and the boy's body was found 100 yards from the home. It was believed he was killed by Apache Indians. Some believe it was the work of the Apache Kid.

In mid-April 1978, 86 years later, Manuel Valdez had begun new employment at the JF Ranch working on repairing broken fences. On April 22nd, Valdez was shot by high-powered rifles and killed instantly. His body was taken and partially buried, presumably by whoever shot him. Billy Martin Jr his employee, had searched for Valdez. But it was Valdez's loyal dog who had found the body weeks later.[1]

* * *

Over the last month, Sarah had gotten fond of taking her brother on hikes. He never got tired or whined. If anything, he moved too quickly for her, but usually never wandered too far.

He also would research and make suggestions on trails to take. Some were trails she hadn't heard of, so she appreciated his excitement. The other day he came to her with three different trails, all new to her. They all seemed a bit much, but she made a deal that if she selected one and they found it too difficult, she would make the call to turn back.

They planned on driving out to the Woodbury trailhead. From Route 60 they would drive forty-five minutes down a series of primitive roads. Once they got to the trailhead, they headed up about half a mile before reaching Woodbury Cabin which intersected different trails. If they continued north, they would eventually end up at the Rogers Canyon Cliff Dwellings but Sarah already told her brother a six-mile hike one way was too much. Maybe some other time, but she wasn't comfortable with the two of them headed out that deep alone.

So when they got to Woodbury Cabin they would head east down Fraser Canyon. Freddy had shared the stories of two murders at the JF Ranch almost 100 years apart.

"Freddy, you didn't tell me there were two murders there," Sarah said.

"We're not going there, although I think the path comes close. I think the ranch is fully operational now." Freddy said.

The two continued for another two miles. Freddy thought that he saw a small cabin on the north side of the trail.

"Hey, look at that!" Freddy said as he went off the trail and headed for it.

"Freddy wait. That might be someone's home." Sarah said as she started to follow Freddy.

As Freddy got closer he saw a small coral comprised of hundreds of vertically large branches. To the rear of it was a smaller structure, which Freddy headed towards.

Sarah knocked on the door of the cabin just in case someone was around. No answer and looking through the window, it looked like the building was vacant for some time.

Freddy pulled on the front door of the small structure and to his surprise, it opened up. It was dark in there, but Freddy entered.

Sarah was still at the main cabin as she circled it. Sarah felt it best to keep moving and not overstay in case the owner of the property or someone else came around. "Freddy let's keep going. This cabin might belong to someone, and I think we've been here long enough."

Sarah turned but didn't see her brother anywhere. She headed to the coral and saw his footprints but no Freddy.

"Freddy, Freddy, let's go. Where are you?" She shouted as she ran frantically around the property.

Freddy came out of the small structure. He turned quickly to where Sarah was. "That wasn't you back there," he gestured to his sister, then back to the building. "Then who did I just see?"

"Is there someone here?" Sarah asked.

"I'm not sure, might be," Freddy paused, "Maybe it was reflection through the window on the mirror. Never mind." as he saw his sister get worried.

"Like I said, someone might own this place, let's keep going," Sarah said as she headed to the trail.

The two kept going but Freddy kept looking back, back past his sister, as he felt there might be someone following them. After a mile, the two of them stopped to take a drink of water.

Freddy continued to scan the area, as he felt certain they were being watched. Eventually, his sister caught his eye.

"Freddy, what is it?" she asked.

"I think we are being watched," Freddy continued. "I think since we were at the cabin. Maybe not, just a feeling."

"Then let's head back, now!" Sarah said.

They both turned and started back on the trail. Their quick pace became a slow jog. Sarah thought she heard something and turned back and fell. What she heard next was not a person behind her, but a rattlesnake to her side.

"Sarah, don't move," Freddy screamed.

Sarah looked at the rattlesnake six feet from her. "What do I do?" she cried.

"Stay still. Maybe it will leave." Freddy said, trying to calm his sister and himself down.

The two waited for the rattlesnake to move. For Sarah, it seemed like an eternity. The snake just stayed coiled, rattling its tail.

"Freddy, I can't just stay here," she whispered, as she knew any noise could send the snake into striking her.

"I'll go down the path just a hundred yards and scream for help. I don't think that will upset the snake from that distance," Freddy said.

Just then, a young man, not much older than Freddy, jumped from behind a rock with a forked rod and in one swift movement pinned down the front of the snake.

Sarah, seeing the snake pinned down, got up and ran to her brother's side. The young man used the stick to send the snake off and then turned to Sarah and Freddy.

"You should be careful out here. It can be dangerous," the young man said.

Sarah and Freddy were both still in shock as they sized up the young man. His clothes appeared homemade and a bit tired. Even his shoes appeared to be homemade, like nothing the two had seen before.

Freddy looked at the young man. "Thank you. You're pretty good with that stick. Didn't I see you before?" Freddy paused. "On another trail."

"I believe so." The young man replied.

"Do you live around here?" Sarah asked.

"Yes. I live in the mountains." He replied.

"Do you live at the cabin we were at?" Sarah continued.

"No. I live somewhere else, but that cabin is not a good place to be. Evil lives there," the young man replied.

The young man heard some noise from over his shoulder, then turned back to them. "You should leave now. Quickly leave."

Sarah and Freddy looked at each other and nodded to the young man and ran back down the trailhead to where their truck was. The young man stood and watched the two disappear on the horizon.

Sarah and Freddy didn't say a word to each other for the next thirty minutes as they made it to the truck and down the primitive road. After they were clear from the trailhead Sarah slammed her brakes, and the truck stopped and she began to cry.

"Freddy, we are never going back there again!" she screamed.

"But the ruins are off that trail," Freddy said, looking disappointed.

"I don't give a shit. We are never going there. Together, alone, ever. Do you understand me?" Sarah said as she took the truck out of park and headed to the main road.

* * *

It became a busy weekend as several hikers were injured or in need in the Superstitions over the weekend. Cal was out to Battleship Mountain to help a few climbers who got into trouble.

Battleship Mountain stands majestically along the LaBarge and Boulder Canyons. From a distance, it appears to be an enormous mountain, as you scale over 2000 feet in elevation, you find at the top narrow sections, which call for scrambles with vertical drops of over 500 feet. Not ideal for someone with a fear of heights.

Periodically, hikers make it to the top and then panic. Cal was airlifted to the base of Battleship, where he climbed to the top to help the hiker. It was a middle-aged woman and her husband was with her, but she didn't feel safe going down with him.

Cal brought a harness, helmets, and rope. He placed the couple on the line a showed them that even if they slipped, the roped would keep them from falling more than a few feet. It was a slow trek down to the base of Battleship Mountain.

Cal made sure they were both hydrated as they all got in the helicopter to get checked out.

Meanwhile, Lil and Shawn McTavish were helping a hiker who fell at the Wave Cave. The Wave Cave had become a popular hike, as it was previously, the cave where the Apache Kid hid out it.

The last several hundred feet are slow gravel and rocks at a 45-degree angle in some places. An older gentleman slipped as he started back down the trail. Lil and Shawn placed him on a wheeled stretcher that was made for these types of trails.

There was also a volunteer Search & Rescue team, sent to the Apache Lake Resort along with an airlift and sheriff backup. A boating accident at the ramp where the trailer became loose, hitting two bystanders.

Waylen Cambrai and a few other volunteers were also busy to the east looking for two lost hikers in the Haunted Canyon.

The hikers had some idea about finding the Dutchman's treasure inside one of the offshoots in the canyon. They were supposed to check in daily with family, but no one had heard from them for two days.

Waylen's group had little to go on. Not sure what provisions the hikers brought with them and what they might expect. Waylen had a team of eleven and they had come through Superior to get to the trailhead.

Air support was also on its way, as there was a lot of ground to cover. Waylen knew of the old Tony Robin cabin and hoped that is where they may have set up camp and left some clues about where they were.

Sure enough, when they got to the cabin, there were some supplies in the cabin, including water, some food, and a few sleeping bags.

Waylen asked one of the other volunteers in the cabin, "Do you see any maps, any notes?"

"No, nothing," a voice from the other side of the room answered.

Waylen stepped outside as the group of volunteers gathered around him. "There are supplies in the cabin, but not sure what they started with," Waylen said as he laid a map on a large boulder. "We'll need to split up. This is a dense canyon. A lot of places they could be and we could end up walking right over them if we aren't looking at everything."

Waylen continued to go on and split up the team with instructions. He heard the new helicopter, Aurora 5, above the canyon, making passes. Waylen radioed them to see if they had any luck, already knowing the answer. He knew this was going to be a long weekend for his team.

After eight hours of combing small offshoots, the two hikers were found. They had run out of water and became disoriented. Aurora 5 picked up the hikers and took them to a hospital. Meanwhile, Waylen and his group had a long walk back as the sun set on them.

* * *

The days were getting longer as summer was approaching. The school year ended and originally Freddy thought he would do a lot of hiking in the mornings before the blistering sun baked the desert.

His sister was spooked last weekend by the rattlesnake and meeting the hiker on the trail. She had said she never wanted to head out that way again and for Freddy, he was disappointed. The Rogers Canyon Cliff Dwellings he had researched were off that trail. Four miles each way so if he was going to see them soon, it would have to be in the next few weeks or wait till the Fall when the temperatures came down again.

Freddy was going to have to convince Sarah that there was nothing to be concerned about. He knew that with every passing week, the rattlesnakes were becoming more active. Freddy rode his bike to the grocery store near his house to get some snacks as he planned on overlooking the Sun setting on the Superstitions.

Freddy purchased a sports drink and a chocolate bar and went to reposition himself in the lot with a good view of the mountains and enjoy the sunset. As he kept one eye on the Superstitions, he watched the people go in and out of the store. He had noticed a Tonto Rangers pickup close by in the parking lot. He had been thinking that becoming a Ranger would be something he would want to do when he was older.

As the sun set on the Superstitions, the mountain took on a pink hue. The shadows became more pronounced, and the mountain took on a mysterious look. As he turned back to the lot, he saw a ranger headed to the pickup. He realized it was the ranger they had met before.

Freddy raised his hand as Lil got closer. "Hello, do you remember me?" Freddy asked.

"You look familiar, give me a hint," Lil said as she smiled back at him.

"You helped my sister and her friend at the Peralta trailhead. My sister and I went back to look for her SD card and you found it," Freddy said excitedly.

"Of course. How is your sister's friend? Feeling better, were her pictures all good?" Lil replied.

"Yeah, I think she is better. I'm guessing her photos ended up fine. It was dumb luck you had the SD card." Freddy shuffled his feet and then looked up at Lil, "When I'm older I think I'd like to be a Forest Ranger," Freddy continued.

"It's a wonderful career if you like the outdoors," Lil said with a smile.

"Yep, I sure do, and there always seems to be an adventure. Last weekend, we went to Woodbury Trail and Fraser Canyon and my sister got a bit of a scare. Now she doesn't want to go to the Rogers Canyon Cliff Dwelling. I might try to go there by myself if I can figure out how to get to the trailhead."

"Oh, Fraser Canyon? What happened?" Lil inquired.

"I think she was a bit spooked because of the stories I told her about two people being killed there, then she tripped and there was a rattlesnake laying in front of her. Thank God another hiker came out of nowhere to get rid of the snake," Freddy said, getting excited about sharing his story.

"Fraser Canyon is a place you want to be careful. The same goes for the Rogers Canyon Cliff Dwelling. Don't try that alone," Lil raised her eyebrows.

"The guy that was there, although I think he was my age, said the same thing. I think he lives in the Superstitions."

"What makes you say that?" Lil asked as she took a few steps to her truck to place her bag inside.

"His clothes looked different. Maybe homemade. I don't know, he said he lived nearby."

Lil appeared a bit concerned. "There are a few cabins in the mountains. Maybe you're right." Lil pulled out a card from her pocket. "So, you want to be a ranger? That's cool. The first rule is safety. So, if you are set on the Rogers Canyon Cliff Dwelling and have no one to take you there, call me and we'll figure out a time and I'll take you. Deal?" Lil said, handing Freddy the card.

"Really! Yes, it's a deal." Freddy said as he took Lil's card.

Lil pulled away in her truck as Freddy's mind drifted thinking about the natives that lived in these mountains hundreds of years ago.

10

Along with the hot temperature, summer in Arizona meant monsoon season. The low pressure pulls moisture from the Pacific and Gulf of California, bringing higher humidity. This leads to thunderstorms, heavy rains, high winds, dust storms, and flash flooding. Arizona is world renowned for its spectacular lightning shows during the monsoon season.

The Search and Rescue teams in and around the Superstitions are kept busy when the storms blow through the mountains. Education to the public is the key to keeping people safe.

* * *

The band of dark clouds rolled across southern Arizona, in its path, the Superstition Mountains. The sun set and the winds increased dramatically. Although no rain was falling, the sky filled with hundreds of lightning strikes. It was a light show like no man or woman could emulate. The residents of Arizona would appreciate the lights in the sky. It wouldn't matter where you looked. The strikes were all around.

For those near the Superstitions, the mountains would flicker with the lightning bolts. In dry seasons, there would be concerns about lightning starting fires, so eyes were focused on the mountains.

The next morning, the mountains escaped a fire the night before, but the forecast called for winds of over 60 miles per hour. With it was expected micro-bursts of rain, which would lead to flash flooding.

Cal's team, the local sheriff's office, park rangers, and the media all did their job to make sure everyone was aware. Specific areas would get more flash floods than others, so the locals knew when to stay away. It was the common person who came out to the Superstitions on a sunny morning, not realizing they needed to keep one eye on the skies.

The hot desert air became cooler, and the humidity picked up. Cal was on the phone with the offices as they tracked a large cell headed directly to the Superstitions. Tonto Rangers warned hikers to watch the sky and to be cautious when they are in the mountains, especially if they are not on higher ground and not prepared for heavy rain.

Cal drove out to the Sheriff's depot in Gold Canyon as he could be closer to potential problem areas. By early afternoon, the cell had intensified. The Maricopa

Sheriff's Department was closing Route 88 to Canyon Lake and Tortilla Flat. They were giving those who were there the choice to leave before the road was fully closed or a second choice to stay and wait out the storm.

And when the storm hit, like always, it came fast and furious. Two to three inches of rain an hour would fall in one area and a hundred feet away wouldn't see a drop until the flash floods came.

Cal looked at the rain coming down. Had his radio in one hand and another eye on the television that had the radar.

A few other deputies were with Cal, ready to assist. "Cal, that's a lot of red," as he nodded to the radar on the television.

"There is. It's a big storm, but we had ample warning. Hopefully, most people are in a safe place." Cal responded.

As if on cue, the radio came to life. "A vehicle is stuck in flood waters in Apache Junction at the foot of the Superstitions." The radio went on with more specific details as Cal and his team got their gear ready and headed to their trucks. Cal had the dispatch to see if the local fire department could send a truck and ladder if needed.

When Cal got to the intersection, he saw the small vehicle had stalled in the flood waters. Cal got as close to the water as possible, instructing the driver to roll down their windows.

"How many people are in the vehicle?" Cal yelled over the noise of the rushing waters.

"Just me," came a voice from inside the car.

"Okay, if your seat belt isn't already off, do so and climb out the window and get onto the roof of your car," Cal yelled to the driver.

The water was getting higher and rushing faster. Cal knew he only had minutes before the car would be carried away. He turned as he saw the firetruck pull up as close as possible and the ladder was on its way to the driver.

Cal smiled at how efficient the fire department was as they helped the driver off his car.

The young man yelled to Cal as they headed to shore. "I'm sorry. I didn't think it was that deep. Thank you." he looked down unable to make eye contact.

"It always looks shallower than it is. Do me a favor, never cross a flooded area." Cal said with a warm smile, as he knew the young man was embarrassed at his mistake.

"No sir, I never will."

Once on shore, a paramedic took the driver into an ambulance to make sure they were fine.

* * *

As Cal approached, he could hear that another call was coming in on the radio. Folks living in Apache Junction near the tip of the Superstitions were seeing the flash floods crest above normal flood levels.

One of the sheriff's trucks had some sandbags. Cal figured he would join in as having as many hands as possible was crucial. Sure enough, as they approached the address, they could see two homes on the south side of the street where the flash flood was closing in on the homes.

Cal could hear on the radio a dispatch for more sandbags as he got out of the truck to help place the bags near the first home. Although the rain had stopped, the flood waters wouldn't crest for another few hours. More bags would be needed.

Cal headed across the street to the second home as they waited for more sandbags. The water was inches away from the foundation as the truck pulled up and dumped sand and another pickup followed, filled with bags and shovels.

In the next hour, the team filled and placed bags to save the two properties. Thankfully, there were no other emergencies, except one on a trailhead that Lil was taking care of. Cal knew it was covered and he would head over after he was through here.

* * *

The rescue Lil was taking care of in the Superstitions was two hikers on the Lost Gold Mine Trail who couldn't get back in time before the water levels increased. They had to cross the creek, but it became a raging river.

Lil and Shawn McTavish were at the Hieroglyphic Trailhead when the call came in as Lil pulled out the rope and headed down the trail. Waylen Cambrai and a few on his team were at the Peralta Trailhead in case an issue arose there.

Waylen heard over the radio that Lil was on her way but figured he could come from the other side and see what happened. He wasn't exactly sure where on the trail the hikers were as creeks popped up all over when heavy rains came. All he knew is he wanted to get to the hikers before Lil did.

Lil and McTavish got to Turks Cap Hill, and she had a feeling the couple was close to Mushroom Rock which wasn't much farther ahead. She wasn't sure what side of the creek they were on and if their car was in Peralta's or Hieroglyphics' parking lot. She knew there were still two cars in the lot when they left.

As the two of them got closer, they heard voices ahead.

"Lil, I think we found them," McTavish said, turning back to Lil.

Lil nodded as they went over the ridge to see the two hikers on the other side of a flash flood. On the other side, with Waylen Cambrai.

"Good afternoon, Ranger McTavish and oh, Lil, you're there too!" Waylen smirked.

"Shawn, we have a rope tied securely to the tree on this side. If you secure the other end over there," Waylen pointed to a large tree near Lil. "We can tie them to the line and they can zip line right over the creek."

Lil looked at how fast the water was raging. "Waylen, maybe it's best to take them back with you and drive them around."

"They're exhausted and they want to get back to their car. If one of you knows how to tie the line properly, it won't be an issue," Waylen snickered.

"It's an unnecessary risk, Waylen," Lil said.

"Ma'am," the hiker interjected. "We'd prefer to come across if that's okay."

Waylen tossed the line to McTavish, "Do you know how to tie it on your end?" Waylen asked, knowing he did.

"I'm good, Waylen," McTavish said as he secured the rope to the large tree behind Lil.

The first hiker was tied to a rope and placed on a portable pulley and lifted her legs over the water as Lil caught her.

The pulley was sent back, and the second hiker was secured to it and pushed toward Lil. As he was halfway across, the rope loosened up behind him and he fell close to the water. He lifted his legs higher, but the movement made the rope fall even farther until he fell into the water.

Lil and McTavish quickly grabbed the rope and threw a short rope at him and pulled him to shore. The two hikers were relieved to be on the other side of the flood waters.

"Shawn, go ahead and take them to the trailhead. I'll untie the ropes." Lil said as she started working on the line.

She tossed the line towards Waylen. "That was a fucking cowboy move," as she lifted both her middle fingers at Waylen.

Waylen pulled the ropes in and laughed.

* * *

The following evening hundreds of more lightning strikes with no rain. Cal went to Lil's since she had a perfect view of the west side of the Superstitions and he keep an eye as if a lightning strike started a fire.

Cal sat outside on the patio with his chair turned to the mountains. Lil brought out another beer for Cal and handed it to him.

"So, was all this Chinese food to soften me up?" Lil continued. "You know, I don't think Waylen did the right thing. His issue with me is going to get someone hurt."

"I agree," Cal said, sipping the beer. "I've asked him right out what his issue is with you. He said he doesn't know. I know we can't have him doing that."

"Did I tell you about the kid in the parking lot? He wants to be a Ranger and were going to go the Cliff Dwelling near Rogers Canyon." Lil said.

"No, you didn't. That's cool. When are you going?" Cal asked.

"Tomorrow, if nothing comes up," Lil said with a big smile. "He seemed determined to go out there and I didn't want him out there by himself."

"Lucky him. He gets a one-on-one guide." Cal laughed.

"Excuse me, I gave you a solo hike when you first started!" She laughed.

The two sat watching the lightning show for an hour, making comments about some of the larger ones.

Then something else caught Cal's eye. "Look at those lights again." Cal started counting quietly to himself and after a few minutes. "Different cadence this time, but starting the same pattern again."

"Are you sure?" Lil asked.

"Look, count the light bursts. One-two-three, one-two, one-two, three," Cal went on until it repeated. "And back to one-two-three."

"Well, maybe. But it could be anything. Some hikers have a code on conditions." Lil said.

"Maybe, but I would think that you would know about it," Cal laughed.

"I must be getting old," Lil snickered back.

* * *

The next morning, the weather was ideal for a hike and things were quiet. Lil had texted Freddy and she met him at the supermarket parking lot. They placed his bike into her truck and headed for the Woodbury trailhead.

"You told your parents where you were going," Lil asked.

"Yes. I almost didn't tell my sister though. I was afraid she was going to talk my parents out of letting me go," Freddy answered.

Lil's truck turned off Route 60 onto the primitive road. Freddy seemed to see so many different things this time than when he came with his sister.

"So when you and your sister were out here and you said you saw someone who lived in the mountains?" Lil asked.

"Yeah, he said he lived close by but didn't say where. He spooked my sister, telling us it was dangerous and we should leave." Freddy answered.

"I would agree a bit. You have to respect the Superstitions and shouldn't go wandering out alone in them. How did he look, I wonder if I know him." Lil continued.

Freddy went on to describe him as best as possible, but he seemed to forget specific features. "I'm sorry. Not much, except he was probably my age. I think he was a Native American. His clothes were ripped, hmm, that's about it."

"Well, a lot of Native Americans lived in these mountains. That's why we're here to see one of the ancient dwellings." Lil continued.

As they drove down road 172, Freddy saw Lil was not headed to the Woodbury Trailhead any longer. "I thought we go to Woodbury?" Freddy asked.

"We're going to Rogers Trough. You need a four-wheel drive, so a lot of people start at Woodbury." Lil explained.

"So no Woodbury today," Freddy said.

Lil looked at a loss for a second, "Hmm, no. We'll stay away from there. Probably not a good place to be."

"That's what the kid we saw said," Freddy said as he looked out the window at the thick vegetation of the desert.

The road became very steep and the four miles took some time, but eventually, they pulled up to the Rogers Trough trailhead.

They started up the Reavis Ranch Trail for a little over a mile until they reached the Rogers Canyon trail, which followed the stream in the canyon. They crossed the stream over and back a few times until they reached the cliff dwellings.

Freddy's eyes lit up as he approached the ruins.

"Freddy, this dwelling was built by the Salado over 600 years ago." Lil continued. "Not much of it is left, but it probably was about 65 rooms and 100 people lived here."

"Wow, my sister is going to be so upset she didn't come out with me to see this," Freddy said as he continued to take pictures with his phone.

*   *   *

Sarah went to visit Jennifer in the morning. Since Jennifer's fall, she had no interest in hiking, although she missed the opportunity of some incredible scenes in the Superstitions.

When Sarah got to Jennifer's house, Jennifer's dad welcomed her in. "Sarah, how are you? I don't see you much anymore," the older, stocky man said.

"Mr. Daniels. I know. I know with school, a part-time job, doing some hiking, my time fills up." Sarah replied as she followed Jennifer's father into the house.

"I barely see my own daughter lately, so I get it. With hiking, you should be careful. I'm always listening to the scanner," Mr. Daniels continued as he nodded to the shortwave radio he had on the small desk in the corner of the living room.

"I am. I remember listening to some calls with you when I was younger." Sarah said as she turned when Jennifer entered the living room.

"Sarah, did I ever show you the pictures from the hike?

"No, you never did, except the one you had online," Sarah said, wondering how long this was going to take to go through all the pictures. Not exactly what she wanted to do this morning.

Jennifer reached for her tablet. I can't believe the ranger had the SD card."

Jennifer started swiping the pictures with a slight monologue for each picture. "Weird thing is, a few pictures are missing," Jennifer said as she continued to swipe. "Right here, I'm missing three pictures. Looks at the file names, goes from 781 to 785."

"You must have deleted them on the trail" Sarah questioned Jennifer.

"I guess so, but I don't remember doing that," Jennifer said as she kept moving from one photo to the other.

Sarah was looking at the photos, but she was listening to Mr. Daniels' scanner radio as it was picking up some calls.

"These were some photos I took a few days after the hike," Jennifer continued, but Sarah was listening more intently to the scanner.

The scanner crackled in the background. "Woodbury… body…" came over the radio, but the reception wasn't very good.

Sarah turned to Mr. Daniels. "Did they say Woodbury Trail?"

"I think that's what I heard," he replied as he tried to adjust the dials on the scanner.

Sarah looked back at Jennifer, "Freddy went hiking with that ranger there this morning." Sarah said as she pulled out her cell phone to call her brother. It went right to voicemail.

"I got to go," Sarah said as she made her way out the door.

"Sarah, where are you going?" Jennifer said, following her out the door.

"I'm going to drive to the Woodbury Trailhead, or at least make my way up there until the little shit answers his phone," Sarah said as she raced to her small pickup.

"Let me go with you. I'll keep dialing as you're driving." Jennifer said as she got into the truck.

* * *

The call came in that a body was found off the Woodbury Trail. Cal made his way up the trail and he could see the area was taped off. One of the Tonto Rangers had got there first, once two hikers reported coming across a body.

"Deputy Ligai," the ranger said as he placed his hand out. "Rod Broker," he continued.

"Yes. We met a few months ago," Cal replied.

"Yes sir. I wasn't sure if you remembered. Anyway, I taped the area off, not that anyone will be headed up here, well, except us," Rod replied.

"You're probably right, but let's not take any chances. What do we have here?" Cal answered.

"It looks like the body has been here for years. In this environment and heat, it's hard to tell how long. There was no identification on the body. Odd."

Cal looked over the body and the ranger was correct. The body was pretty much decomposed and more of a partially clothed skeleton.

"I think you're right. Odd that there is no identification on them. I'll get a forensic team up here. Hopefully, the dental records might help," Cal said as he picked up his radio and called in a forensic team. He wasn't expecting something like this. Cal stood and scanned the area. These Superstitions had taken another life. Cal couldn't help but wonder was the remains here were one of the three he was looking for.

Within a few hours, a forensic team was looking over the area. They took pictures and examined the body before transporting it.

11

A year and a half after Adolf Ruth went missing in the Superstitions, an electrician, Tex Bradford from Globe, Arizona, went into the Superstition Mountains looking for the lost gold mine. No one knows if he met the same fate as Adolf Ruth, as he was never seen again.[1]

* * *

Sarah and Jennifer were headed to the Woodbury trail. Sarah had Jennifer calling her brother on his cell phone along the way, but he probably would not answer.

"Sarah, are we going to look for him? We don't have any water, walking sticks, anything," Jennifer said.

"Actually, my boots and walking sticks are in the truck. The sneakers I'm wearing are fine. We wear the same size so you can wear them. And I have some water in the back here. Probably warm, but I always have water with me." She said as they maneuvered down the primitive road.

As they approached the trailhead, there were several sheriff's vehicles and the SAR truck.

She parked her pickup quickly and jumped out, running to the trailhead. Jennifer was trying to keep up but couldn't. Sarah heard a helicopter, then saw it rise over the horizon.

"Freddy!" Sarah cried.

As she focused on the helicopter, a Tonto Ranger came up to her. "I'm going to have to ask you to leave. This trail is going to be closed for the rest of the day, maybe tomorrow, too."

"My brother. My brother Freddy. Is that him in the helicopter?" Sarah cried.

"I really can't share anything with you at this time," the ranger said as Cal approached the two.

"This young lady is looking for her brother," the ranger said.

"Freddy. My brother is Freddy Campbell Is he injured badly?" Sarah asked.

"The person in the helicopter is not your brother," Cal continued, hoping she would calm down. "You say he is hiking here?"

"Yes, he went to the cliff dwellings. He went with a female ranger we met a few weeks back." Sarah said, gaining her composure.

As they talked, more vehicles pulled up as a small group, including Waylen Cambria, who walked came up the trail.

Waylen walked up to Cal. "Not sure if you need any help. If anything needs to be secured off?" he asked.

Cal forced a smile of acknowledgment. "No, we are all set," as he turned back to Sarah. "So your brother is probably with Ranger Shanta."

"Yes, that's her name," Jennifer piped in.

"I can't get him on my cell phone. I realize he is probably out of range," Sarah said.

"What happened?" Waylen asked the two girls, finally staring at Jennifer.

Cal turned to Waylen. "A couple of hikers found the remains of a body. And these two young ladies are looking for their brother, Freddy, you said." Cal said as he looked at Sarah.

"Yes, Freddy. I heard something on the scanner. I thought Freddy was hurt. After what happened here the other week, I guess I panicked." Sarah said, trying to gain her composure.

"What happened the other week?" Waylen inquired.

"My brother and I were hiking. We were in Fraser Canyon on Woodbury Trail for a bit. I fell and there was a rattlesnake a few feet from me," Sarah answered.

"That will scare just about everyone," Waylen said.

"Just spooky, at least to me, and a boy about the age of my brother came out of nowhere and flicked the snake away. Then he told us we shouldn't be there, at least alone."

Cal Picked up his radio. "Well, the young man is probably right. Let me see if I can get Ranger Shanta. See exactly where they are."

Cal turned away from the group and radioed Lil, "Lil, it's Cal. Are you near the Woodbury Trail or in Rogers Canyon?"

There was no answer, so Cal repeated the message. He saw the group talking and wanted to get back to them.

Finally, Lil replied, "Cal, I'm here, I'm in Rogers Canyon.'

"With the kid?" Cal replied.

There was a long silence, then Lil replied. "He was with me."

"Was?" Cal replied.

"I took him to the cliff dwelling here in the canyon. He went around the back of one of the structures and," Lil paused, "He disappeared."

"Shit. Well, his sister is here at the Woodbury trailhead, where we just found a body."

"I thought I heard that. With the kid here, I turned the volume down on the radio."

"I have several people with me. It's too hot to be out there any longer than you already have been. We might as well all help look for him. Your buddy Waylen is one of them. We'll see you shortly." Cal said as he signed off.

Cal headed to the group to tell them what Lil shared with him over the radio.

"Freddy better be okay or I'll kill that ranger," Sarah screamed.

"We'll find him. You and your friend stay here," Cal said.

"No way. If you make me stay, I'll just circle around and search on my own." Sarah said, as her adrenaline increased.

Cal knew there was no way to talk this young lady and her friend out of looking for her brother. "Okay, stay with me. Get in my truck and we'll drive up to the next trailhead."

They all started walking up to their vehicles as Waylen walked up to Cal. "I'm telling you. Something isn't right with your girl. Not sure what it is, but she seems to be around a lot with shit like this. Just saying," as Waylen headed with a few of his team to another pickup truck.

*   *   *

Lil heard the radio go dead. Cal had known she was with Freddy going out to the cliff dwelling. Freddy's sister was here and now Cal was headed her way with Waylen.

Lil was enjoying the morning with Freddy. He had done a lot of research on the Superstitions and the native people who had lived here. It was invigorating to see his excitement. He had brought a small camera and asked smart questions. They had discussed the people that had lived here and together went through a majority of the rooms.

Lil knew about the body off the Woodbury Trail and didn't want to have Freddy distracted. Her radio had gone off a few times, but she turned the volume down if it pertained to the situation not too far from them.

Lil's radio went off as she and Freddy were in one of the great rooms in the center of the ruins. Lil heard the initial message and knew she had to respond.

"Freddy, I have to take this. It shouldn't be long. I'll be back in a few minutes." Lil said as she walked out to the front of the ruins.

"Okay, I'll be in the room over here in back," he said as he went through a small doorway to a small room in the back.

When she got off the radio, she returned to the small room where Freddy had said he would be. He was no longer there, and she searched the surrounding rooms.

"Freddy. Freddy, where are you?" she called out.

He was nowhere to be found. She backtracked her steps and began looking in every room they had been in earlier. She continued to call out for him. Then the radio came alive. It was Cal.

She knew in less than an hour the group would be up at the ruins. She desperately wanted to find Freddy, find him before the group arrived.

* * *

Freddy was engrossed in the old ruins. His mind couldn't fathom that hundreds of Native Americans lived in these broken-down homes. Lil had given him so much information on the way up, so many things he wasn't aware of.

When they got to the ruins, she continued to talk about the people who lived there. She told him to feel free to explore but not to walk on any of the roofs, take home any artifacts, and be careful along the walls, as many of them were very brittle.

Freddy had headed to a small room in the back. He noticed Lil was still out in front and talking on her radio, so he figured his question could wait till he made his way out. Freddy saw a small hole in the floor in the far corner. He walked over and bent over to get a good look. He wasn't sure what it was used for, another question for Lil, he thought.

He stood up and turned around and standing in the room was the young boy that he and his sister had seen the other week on the Woodbury Trail. The young man placed his finger to his lips, telling Freddy to be quiet. He pointed at Freddy, then himself, and then to a small opening in the far wall.

The young boy quickly lifted himself into the opening, then reached back to help Freddy up. At first, Freddy couldn't see much except the silhouette of the young boy in front of him. The two of them crawled about 100 feet and then Freddy could see more light and the passageway got larger where they could stand.

"My name is Freddy," he eventually said to the young man.

The young man turned. "My name is Naiche. I've been watching you over the last few months. I want to show you something. It will be a secret."

"Of course, but I have to get back. The ranger will be looking for me. I've already probably been gone too long." Freddy realized just how long he really had been gone.

"Don't worry about the ranger. I will get you back to her soon. I've met her before. She will understand." Naiche said with confidence.

"Well, just a bit longer. I really feel bad leaving her," Freddy said.

"We are almost there. Remember, this is a secret. You can tell no one." Naiche said as he looked into Freddy's eyes.

"I swear. I won't tell anyone." Freddy replied.

The two walked to where the light was coming from. "Okay Freddy, look," Naiche said as an enormous smile appeared on his face as his hand reached out in front.

Freddy's eyes followed the movement of Naiche's arm and Freddy's eyes grew in wonderment.

* * *

The Sun was settling in the sky and the temperature was dangerous to be out this long. If Lil didn't find Freddy soon, the search would become more challenging. Lil had checked the cliffs below for Freddy just in case he had slipped past her earlier and she had missed him.

Cal had radioed her a few minutes away and so in her mind, she wanted to split the group up and look throughout the ruins and the surrounding area.

She heard the voices approaching. Waylen seemed to be the loudest. Cal was in front with Waylen and it looked like another four or five people, including the two young girls she had helped a few months back.

"Lil, any luck finding the young boy, Freddy, is it?" Cal asked, realizing the answer.

"No. I've searched every room here, the cliffs. He just disappeared." Lil continued as she looked at Sarah, "Has he ever just taken off?"

Sarah looked at Lil, not sure what was going on. "Not really. He usually stuck by me," Sarah said with a discouraged smile.

"The sun is going to set soon," Waylen chimed in. "Let's split up and see what Ranger Shanta missed."

Cal quickly stepped in. "Okay Lil, you've been here searching for him. I'm sure you've played this out. Where should we start?"

"Let's see, there are eight of us. Let's divide into four groups." Lil continued. I'll go with Freddy's sister, and we'll hit the far end of the ruins. Cal, if you take their friend and look at the other end. Waylen, why don't two of you search below the cliff and two above? Maybe somehow he got up on top."

"Let's get a move on. Let's keep in contact." Cal said as the group split up.

"Sarah, right?" Lil asked, knowing the answer.

"Yes, that's right."

"Your brother seemed to enjoy his time here. Then I answered the radio and he was gone." Lil said, hoping to get a reaction from Sarah.

"I can't say he stays at my side, but he has never taken off. I hope he didn't fall somewhere." Sarah replied.

"Don't worry, I'm sure we'll find him," Lil said.

At the other end of the ruins, Cal and Jennifer were meticulously going through each room, calling out for Freddy. Cal wasn't happy that Sarah and Jennifer were here, but he knew if he left them behind, they would go off on their own and they could then be looking for three kids instead of one.

Cal could tell that Jennifer was tired and he didn't want to push her limits too far, as they still had a far walk back.

"Look Jennifer, I think you need a rest. If we go out front, will you stay there until someone comes back? I don't need to be looking for anyone else," Cal said, looking into the young girl's tired eyes.

"I promise. My feet are killing me. It's really hot. I think I need to just sit for a few minutes." She said to Cal.

"No, not for a few minutes. Until I get back. Do you understand?" Cal said as they walked to the front of the cliff dwelling, looking for a place for Jennifer to sit.

"Deal," Jennifer said as she sat on a rock near the front entrance.

Waylen and a few other volunteers were searching above and below the cliff dwelling. Checking to make sure Freddy hadn't fallen and was unconscious in the vegetation. The team below had a slower time, as there was some heavy brush below. Waylen had climbed up the cliff above the dwelling with another member of his team. He hadn't expected to find anything up there but hoped more that from that vantage point, he might spot Freddy.

Sarah was getting more discouraged as each minute went by. She knew her brother wouldn't just take off.

"How could my brother just disappear? I don't get it. You know this place. I don't see how that could happen," Sarah said as she became more impatient.

"I know we are going to find him, but I'm baffled a bit too," Lil said as she pushed aside a large bush and looked under it.

"Sarah, your brother was telling me about the other week on the Woodbury Trail," Lil said, turning to Sarah. "He said there was a young boy that helped the two of you?"

"It was kind of weird, the whole thing. First, the snake and then this strange boy," Sarah said as she glanced along the side of the trail, hoping to spot her brother.

"Strange? What was strange about him?" Lil asked.

"I don't know. We think he lives in the mountains. He looked a little dirty and he had old clothes. I don't know how to describe it, just weird." Sarah answered.

"I don't think any young boys are living in the mountains. Maybe he was camping," Lil smiled back at Sarah as they continued to comb the brush around the dwelling.

They continued to walk a bit until they heard Waylen's voice. "We found him. Over here."

Sarah ran to where the voice was. She saw the group huddled around something in front of the ruins. Cal, Jennifer, and the other volunteers were there. As Sarah got closer, Jennifer turned to her.

"It's Freddy," she stepped aside, and Sarah could see her brother in the middle of the group. "He said he got lost." Jennifer continued.

Freddy turned to his sister. "Sorry, I got disoriented. I went off in the wrong direction, hoping I would find Ranger Shanta."

Cal placed his hand on Freddy. "As long as you are okay. That's what's important."

Sarah looked at her brother. She knew he didn't get lost, not him. She would figure out what was going on later. Right now, she just wanted to get home. She walked up to her brother and wrapped her arms around him.

"You had me worried. You had us all worried."

Cal turned to the group. "Okay, make sure everyone takes a drink. This is too hot to be out in the afternoon. Once we are all good we'll get going. This hike is easier in the daylight."

The group headed back down the trail to their vehicles as the Sun and shadows of the Superstitions gave the mountains a mysterious feel.

Cal walked next to Freddy and Sarah. "Freddy, you sure you're okay?"

Freddy continued to walk. "Yes, sir, I'm fine."

Cal continued to talk to the young man. "Can you tell me what happened? I need to fill some paperwork out."

"I was in the far small room and then when I saw Ranger Shanta on her radio, I went to check out some of the paintings along the lower cliff. I slipped and fell. I guess I took off in the wrong direction and got a bit distracted. I turned around and backtracked my steps." Freddy explained.

"And when you came back, you came up along the base of the cliff and then headed to the small room you were in?" Cal asked.

"Yeah, that sounds right," Freddy answered.

"I'm just surprised you didn't see the men down there searching for you." Cal continued.

"I saw them, but I saw a few people in the dwellings, so that's where I went. I was looking for Ranger Shanta." Freddy said, keeping his eyes on the trail.

Cal turned back to Lil, who was walking behind them. "Lil, I'll touch base with you tomorrow for any information I don't have."

Lil nodded and was trying to figure out how her day turned out like this. She takes a boy out on a hike and he gets lost when he was with her. She was already thinking about getting home to take a long bath. The Cliff Dwelling in Rogers Canyon was one of her favorite places and now she had an airy feeling about it.

Sarah listened to Cal and her brother and knew that Freddy was lying. She would find out what was going on when they got in her pickup. Soon enough, Cal dropped Sarah, Jennifer, and Freddy off at the Woodbury Trailhead. Cal watched them get into Sarah's pickup and then followed them down the primitive road, back to Route 60.

Once they had made their way to Route 60, Cal called Lil on his cell.

"Lil it's Cal. What happened up there?"

"You know I'm trying to figure it all out. This afternoon was like a bad dream. I'm going home, taking a hot bath, then going right to bed. I'll call you in the morning." Lil replied before hanging up the phone.

As Sarah turned up Route 60 and she saw Cal had headed towards Florence, Sarah looked in the rear-view mirror at her brother.

"So   Freddy,   out   with   it.   What happened? Something you didn't want to share with the deputy or ranger?"

"No, nothing happened.   Just like I told the deputy. I went off in the wrong direction. I feel kind of, I don't know, stupid." Freddy said, looking at his sister.

"Well, maybe you're just tired and dehydrated. We can talk about it tomorrow. I'm just trying to figure out what happened on the trail." Sarah said.

Freddy just looked out the pickup window, trying to understand what he had seen a few hours back. He would love to share his encounter with his sister, or maybe Ranger Shanta, but he gave his word to Naiche. He would keep the secret the two of them shared.

12

In 1947, a retired photographer, James Cravey, from Phoenix, Arizona, had a dream about where the lost treasure in the Superstition Mountains was. Cravey had hired a helicopter pilot to take him to a designated spot in the mountains. Cravey brought water, food, and supplies for approximately a week.

The pilot returned days later as Cravey had arranged, but James Cravey never came back. The pilot informed the authorities, but to no avail, they did not find Cravey. Seven months later, two individuals came across a decapitated skeleton. They were the remains of James Cravey.[1]

* * *

Over the next few weeks, there were dozens of SAR volunteers in the Superstition Mountains helping hikers.

Two separate groups of treasure hunters needed people in their group to be airlifted out.

The SAR volunteers, in both cases, could get to the injured parties and stabilize their injuries before the helicopters reached them.   Numerous hikers didn't understand the excessive heat in Arizona and became dehydrated quickly.

Cal had worked closely with the SAR groups as they aided the hikers in the mountains. The Superstition Mountains fell in several counties, so these teams needed to work hand in hand. Maricopa County just north of Pinal shared a good blunt of the accidents in the Superstition Mountains.

Deputy Bracken was the deputy the Cal seemed to work with the most. Cal would begin at the Lost Dutchman State Park and move southward. Deputy Bracken would cover the north of the park and further into the area of the lakes along the Salt River.

With all the manpower, nothing could cover extensive areas and difficult terrains like a helicopter. Calling in a helicopter to transport injured hikers to safety was monumental.

Having obtained an additional helicopter was coming in handy. The UH-60 Black Hawk had been put to use since its arrival. Deputy Austin and his crew were excited to get the bird out. They had picked up a group of eight hikers that made it to the top of Flatiron but didn't bring enough water to make the journey down. Two were exhausted and dehydrated when the call came in, but by the time the copter landed, they all boarded. The Superstitions were too much for them.

They had picked up numerous hikers who had twisted or broken ankles and legs. The new night vision was put to use a few weeks back when the Border Patrol rented out the helicopter and crew for a night roundup. But its first test for night search was about to take place.

A homing beckon had gone off at dusk near Iron Mountain. Within an hour, the signal was lost, and not knowing the reason, Aurora 5 was sent to look. After the first pass of Iron Mountain, the sun set.

Iron Mountain rewarded those who made it up the steep path with some breathtaking views, including Weavers Needle to the west and to the east the view of the West Fork Pinto Creek. As the sun set, the views disappeared and the mountain was overtaken by its dark shadows and it became a dangerous place to be.

"This is Aurora 5," Deputy Austin radioed in. "It's getting dark here. We will turn on our night vision cameras. You should be able to link up and see them on the monitor at the office."

Deputy Austin hit a view knob and the radio replied, "Affirmative, Aurora 5. We have visual."

Deputy Austin needed to focus on not only what was below him in the search but any abrupt cliffs in front of them. He turned to his co-pilot. "It's dark on the east side here. I need to focus on the mountain. If you see anything, let me know."

The night vision picked up a few longhorn sheep, but they were easy to distinguish. After a few flybys off the path, Austin decided to start a grid starting closest to the path. Within minutes, they came across two people on the ground.

"There they are," Austin said as he circled back at them.

"Yep, they light up like a Christmas tree on these things," came a voice from the back.

"Makes it easier. It's not like we are right over them." Austin replied as he circled back, looking to see if there was a place to land or if they were going to send someone down to retrieve them.

"Chuck, it looks like I'm going to send you down. If we need to send a basket, let me know." Austin continued as he circled the two hikers below.

Chuck went down a line to the two hikers. The one looked to have broken his ankle while the other was frazzled. One by one, the two hikers were lifted to Aurora 5 and then taken to the local hospital.

The following morning, the Maricopa SAR helicopter searched for injured hikers near Fish Creek while Aurora 5 aided boaters at Saguaro Lake. The team airlifted two injured boaters out of the water and got them to medical attention. They weren't back to base for more than an hour when they got a call about a hiker near Hackberry Butte. The hiker became dehydrated and was stranded in the mountains until other hikers came upon him. There was a clearing that enabled Austin Johnson to land his bird and pick up the hiker.

It was a busy weekend but extremely rewarding. As Austin landed Aurora 5 for the evening, he turned to his crew. "Job well done. Is there a better job than this?"

* * *

Lil was busy as well over the last few weeks. Typically, as the heat climbs higher up, there are fewer hikers. The locals go for short hikes in the morning. It's the hikers from out of town who do not know what the afternoon Arizona heat can do to you.

She was at a variety of trailheads throughout the week and would get there at 4 am before the sun rose and before a majority of hikers hit the trails. She would greet the hikers as they made their way onto the trailhead, inquiring how far they intended to go, get a gauge on their experience, and most importantly, how much water they had.

With all her good intentions, she was flagged down by hikers who were returning, letting her know there were hikers in distress. The heat and lack of consumption of water were the most common. Lil would usually head up the trail at least once a day with water and ice packs.

The first hiker in need was a local older gentleman who thought he had a new lead on the lost gold mine. He was overtaken by the heat and a few young hikers tried to help him back to the parking lot, but he was set on finding the gold. When the hikers who wanted to help him got back to the trailhead, they told Lil about the man and she quickly met up with him to take him back.

One day there was a small group from out of town. Lil asked how much water they had and suggested at what point they should think about turning back. Lil knew what that point was and later in the afternoon when she didn't see them return, she headed up the trail. A few miles later she found them out of water and burning in the hot Sun. The next day, another small group of people visiting friends and wanted to hike where the lost gold mine was. Not having much of an idea what they were doing, Lil checked on them earlier in the hike than normal and her hunch was correct. They need some ice packs, cold water, and encouragement to get back to the car lot. It was all part of being a Ranger in the Superstition Mountains in the Arizona summer.

* * *

Cal sat in his office printing out the reports and making sure everything was backed up. It had been a busy six months. The new helicopter was getting a lot of use lately. The sheriff was pleased with his work. His desk was clear except for the folder at the top left corner of his desk which Cal had marked "missing hikers".

Bob Kravis, Michael Kowalski, and Linda Sharper were on top of this list. Another dozen hikers missing with no trace. How many others might be out there? How many others were reported back home like the three he uncovered?

Still, no identification of the skeletal remains that they found a few weeks back near Woodbury

Trailhead. They were hoping the dental records might show up on someone who had gone missing.

Waylen had mentioned a Sandy Davenport but Lil didn't remember her and there was nothing in the database on her. It was like it never happened, or was erased. Early on, Cal saved duplicated files on an external drive that he had under lock and key, and only the sheriff knew of it. He also kept the printer busy, making hard copies, many times taking them home, trying to see if there was a clue buried in them.

Besides that file of missing hikers on his desk, life was good. The job was rewarding. He enjoyed the people he worked with, and his relationship with Lil was going well.

Betty walked past Cal's desk. "Cal, you are so precise with your paperwork and your desk is so neat. You sure could help some other people out," she chuckled.

"I just don't want to lose anything. Make sure everything is in the database and saved." Cal replied.

"Oh, my god! I almost forgot I may have found that one file you were looking for, Sandy Davenport." Betty said as she went back to her desk and brought back a manila folder.

"You are kidding me," Cal said enthusiastically.

"Here it is. Not sure if this is it. The name on it is Dave Sanport. The time frame seems close." Betty continued. "I'll email you the file as well, but I see how you like everything printed."

Cal quickly opened the folder and went through the documents. It was the correct year, but he wasn't sure of the exact date. It was the Reavis Trail and it says that the family called in the next day that she had returned home. Cal thought it looked like a page was missing, which had the hiker's contact information. So two names to look at Sandy Davenport or Dave Sanport.

"Betty, thank you so much. This is great. I'll let you know what I find out. I now have reading material for tonight," Cal chuckled.

He continued to skim through the report and came to a copy of hand-written notes. It was hard to read between the handwriting and photocopy, but he was sure he would figure it out tonight. As he continued to skim his way to the end of the notes, he was surprised to see the signature at the bottom.   The notes were written and signed by Liluye Shanta.

* * *

Sarah was still trying to figure out what her brother had seen weeks back. The first few days after they found him, he had said absolutely nothing. She knew he didn't get lost and for him to not say anything about it, he was hiding something.

It bothered her more that Freddy didn't want to share whatever he was hiding, than knowing something had happened. She tried many times to start up a conversation, but Freddy seemed to be distracted and quickly would walk away.

Finally, Sarah's mother asked her to go to the store and to have Freddy help. Usually, Sarah would be irritated with this, but she would finally have Freddy in her pickup and he couldn't get away.

It only took the first turn around the block for Sarah to turn to her brother.

"Okay, Freddy, what's going on?"

"What? Mom said I have to come with you." Freddy replied.

"You know what I'm talking about. What happened at the cliff dwellings?" She said in a raised voice.

"I told you. I got lost. It was really hot. I slipped and tumbled and when I got up, I headed in the wrong direction. Then I had to double back."

"Bullshit. First, you don't get lost, not you. Second, lost for what, two hours?" Sarah continued.

"I'm not sure what to tell you. Maybe I hit my head and blacked out. It didn't seem like two hours. I'm sorry sis, really," Freddy replied while wishing he could share with her what he saw in the Superstitions.

Sarah dropped the conversation, hoping that he would come around, but he never did. He had not asked her to go hiking and as far as she knew he hadn't gone hiking with anyone else.

She thought about asking him to go hiking, but they were in the middle of summer. The heat, the rattlesnakes, and the overall elements were not conducive for any hiking. She knew her brother had been busy the last few weeks, but didn't say where he was going. Finally, he told her he was going to the local library to find out information on the Native American Indians that had lived in the Southwest. The library had a display of some artifacts that intrigued him and had a few local speakers.

One speaker was a ranger from the Casa Grande Ruins National Monument. The ranger had suggested that he would enjoy the ruins and that some artifacts were of the same time period.

So Freddy approached his sister to ask if she could take him. Sarah realized how funny it was that six months ago she thought her brother was a pain in her side, and now she was excited that he asked her to take him.

It took almost an hour to get to Coolidge, but in the middle of summer, being in a cool pickup was one of the best places to be. As they turned the corner in front of the National Monument, Freddy looked at the large wall that surrounded the grounds.

As they entered through the main gate, they could see a large multi-level ruin that had a cover over it to protect it from the harsh Arizona sun. The small parking lot was almost full but they found a spot in the far corner to park.

The visitor center in front was a small building, but Freddy found it to be fascinating. Sarah looked at her brother. She could tell how excited he was.

* * *

Cal couldn't sleep. He kept thinking about the report Betty found on a Dave Sandport with Lil's notes on it. Was this Sandy Davenport? Either way, Lil didn't mention either name months ago when he had asked about past hikers where the search was called off as they were found at home. He didn't think for a minute that Lil would forget that and again said nothing when he asked the other month, specifically about Sandy Davenport.

Cal knew they were going to have dinner the following night, so he took the report home to go over it and have time to think about what it might mean.

He could tell the handwriting was hers, but it almost appeared that it was sloppy on purpose. It mentioned her looking for the hiker of Reavis Trail and other rangers and volunteers searching other areas. It might be nothing, but it didn't feel right.

Cal drove down Route 60 into Apache Junction where he would pick Lil up and they would go to a little pub in town where they had become regulars. Cal could see some dark clouds forming to the south as he peaked in his rear-view mirror. During the monsoon season, he knew anything could happen.

* * *

Cal and Lil finished dinner and were nursing their last drink. The dinner had been a quieter one than normal.

"Lil, you seem a bit preoccupied. Is everything okay?" Cal asked.

"Just a lot on my mind. Frankly, I was just about to say the same thing to you," Lil replied with a forced smile.

"I think you're right. I wanted to ask you something and was hoping it would just fall into our conversation, but it didn't." Cal continued. "It's about Sandy Davenport."

There was no reaction from Lil as she looked down at her drink. "Or maybe it was Dave Sandport. Does either name ring a bell, Lil?"

Lil looked up at Cal. "That is a name I haven't heard in a long time. I remember Sandy Davenport."

"What do you remember? I would like to know. It might help me out a bit," Cal answered.

"Sure, help you with what?" Lil answered, waiting for Cal to respond. After a few seconds and still, Cal didn't reply.

"She was a hiker that had gone missing. About ten years ago. Is there an update on her?"

"So you remember her now? When I asked you a few months ago about hikers that we search the Superstitions for, and they ended up back at home," Cal said with a bit of anger in his tone.

"I'm sorry, Cal," Lil said as she placed her hands over the table onto his. "Both deputies were involved in a rescue in the southern portion of Pinal County, so Sergeant Broad asked me to take the lead. I was somewhat new. It wasn't my best work. We ended up getting a call from her family that she was home. So I kind of wanted the entire thing to go away. I filed the report so there would be no red flags and I wouldn't have a blemish on my job. It's no excuse. She ended up coming home, so no harm." Lil explained.

"But when I asked you a few months back, you could have told me, explained what happened," Cal said as his tone was more frustrated than angry.

"I was embarrassed. Cal, I didn't want to lose your trust and respect."

"At least now I know about Sandy Davenport, although there was no phone or address to reach out to her. The trust and respect you mentioned now have a bit of a blemish on it, especially with the relationship we have here. You should be able to tell me anything."

"I wanted to tell you a few times, but I didn't know how to. I'm so embarrassed."

"Lil, is there anything else I should know? Better now than later," Cal replied.

"No. It was a mistake. I was young. I shouldn't have done it and I should have told you before now." Lil said as she squeezed Cal's hand.

Cal paid the check and they headed back to Lil's house. Cal turned into her driveway but never turned off the ignition.

"Cal, are you coming in? Aren't you staying over?" Lil asked him.

"I think I'm going to go to my house tonight," Cal replied.

"Cal, are we okay? It was a mistake." Lil said, looking into his eyes.

"Yeah, we are good. I just need a little time alone. I have to absorb this. I'm sure we'll be fine."

Lil opened the car door and headed to her front porch. Cal pulled away, feeling like he was sucker punched. He finally found someone he trusted and cared about. He believed what he told Lil. They would be fine, but tonight it hurt.

13

In approximately 450, the Sonoran Desert people began settling down and started more of a farmer's existence. The Hohokam culture flourished in southern Arizona. Most villages were established in the Salt River and Gila River Valley.

They had developed an irrigation system hundreds of miles long, using the water from multiple rivers, including the Salt River, which had carved through the Superstition Mountains. By 1400, Casa Grande, forty miles south of the Superstitions, became the centerpiece of this civilization.

Trade flourished as Native American tribes from hundreds of miles would come to exchange materials. Their farms produced a surplus to trade for turquoise, seashells, copper bells, and other valuable items.

By that time the Hohokam Indians no longer lived in the Superstitions, but other tribes, the Pima and

Apache, would eventually make the Superstitions their home.

In the late 1300s early 1400s, the great city of Casa Grande was abandoned. Many theories are out there, including drought, disease, and unpredictable weather. Some feel their ties with the Superstitions and mysteries may have played a part. Some say a small group moved back into the Superstitions.

At the same time, the Salado tribe lived in the Superstitions between 1250 and 1450. They were primarily cliff dwellers, but it was believed they left the Superstitions due to severe drought conditions.

* * *

Jeff Albright was hiking deep into the Superstitions. He was packing up his tent and cleaning up his site and was thinking about his hike for the day.

Jeff had decided that since he got off to a late start, the previous day he would pack provisions to camp one night. He had made his way to Rogers Trough Trailhead and then headed down Rogers Canyon. His goal was to check out the cliff dwellings first thing in the morning and then to look for a hidden trail he was told about that few knew of. It would lead to more dwellings, so he was told.

The dwelling was home to the Salados around 1300. The dwelling had survived the elements mainly, as it was constructed partially in a cave. Jeff had been here before and was glad to see that there wasn't any additional graffiti on the walls. He took several pictures, even though he had many from his last visit a few years back.

As he had gone through the dwelling, he forced himself to take his time as he was excited to look for the hidden trail he was told of and to see where it leads to. He packed his camera away and took a few sips of water and headed east, but knew he was to look for a crevice in the cliff shortly after the dwellings. It was supposedly a good five feet above the path and would only allow a thin person in.

Jeff walked the trail along the cliff and didn't come across any crevice that fit the description. He came to Frog Tanks Trail, where he was told, if he made it to Frog Tanks he had gone too far. Frustrated, he turned around and focused his view higher up the cliff wall.

He came across a petroglyph that he felt he had seen a few times today. Two hunters with spears hunting for what looked to be deer or sheep. A large Sun was above the drawing and a larger hunter or warrior. This large warrior was a different color than all the other drawings, he was white.

He saw nothing that a grown man could sliver through and knew he was coming back to the cliff dwellings. Jeff turned around slowly and looked at any imperfections on the cliff wall. He stopped where an ironwood tree was growing on the ledge. Nothing there, but his eyes were drawn to the tree. He followed the tree branches up the cliff and then he saw it. Hidden by a thick branch about fifteen feet up was a small crevice in the wall.

He looked up and down the tree. Was this the place? He looked at all the branches to determine if there was a way to climb up to the opening. After analyzing and finding no clear-cut way, just start it and take one branch at a time.

He found a set of boulders near the tree, and by climbing up them he could step onto a lower branch. As he stopped on the branch, he looked at the opening in the wall and first looked for the shortest route, but soon saw the smaller branches might not hold his weight. The branch to his left seemed to be the largest and sturdiest, although it hung over the cliff, fifty feet straight down if he missed his step. All the equipment on his back wasn't helping.

Jeff placed his left foot on the branch, bouncing it to see how it handled his weight. No creaks or cracks from the branch as he took a step forward with his other foot. Don't look down, he thought, focused on the next branch. He quickly found the next logical branch and moved up closer to the opening in the cliff and a safer place to be. Over the next ten minutes, he worked himself to the opening in the cliff. One last step and he was in the small opening.

He could see that this cave moved upward with light shining through it. Luckily, he had a flashlight and he pulled it out. There were strong vines on both sides and he used the one to his right to pull himself up to the light above. As he made his way to the top, he thought he could hear voices and people moving things around. He picked up his pace. Were there more hikers there? Maybe this wasn't as hidden as he was told.

As he hoisted himself up, he couldn't believe his eyes. Something wasn't right. Was he dreaming? He scanned the area to take it all in. In front of him looked to be a large cave with multiple openings. He knew the Superstitions were formed by volcanos and trapped gases formed caves as the lava cooled, but he had never heard of something this big. But that's not what shocked Jeff. It was what appeared to be numerous structures in the cave. These structures were like the clay brick dwelling he had seen on the previous day, except these were maintained and used! There must have been a hundred people down there.

Jeff took off his backpack and pulled out his camera. He zoomed in on the activity down below. By the way the people were dressed, they appeared to be Native Americans, but their dress wasn't anything Jeff was familiar with. He wanted to get closer to the village below to get more pictures.

He saw a path to his left and slowly walked down it, hoping that no one would see him. He was still high above and there were numerous boulders to hide behind. After fifty feet off to the one side, Jeff stopped to take additional pictures.

What was this? Who were these people? Was it a group of hippies, some type of social experiment or were they native inhabitants of the Superstitions? Jeff continued farther down to get more photos. He was totally in awe of what he saw in front of him. He stumbled for a second and some stones fell to the village below. Jeff hid behind a boulder in case someone below heard the stones.

Sure enough, Jeff's stumble got some attention. "Hello, up there, hello." Came a voice from below.

Jeff stayed behind the boulder, hoping they hadn't seen him. Again the same voice from below said, "You, please come down."

Jeff stayed behind the boulder, still hoping he may not have been seen. But he heard the person coming closer. "We are going to need you to leave that camera behind," came a voice.

Jeff could hear the footsteps of multiple people running in his direction. He wasn't sure if he should run or stay. He only had another minute he figured before the decision would no longer be his, so he stood up and ran back to the entrance he came in through.

In that nanosecond, he thought if they pursued him, running was probably the right choice. If not, he could come back another time, maybe with some friends. This village in the cave wasn't going anywhere.

He maneuvered into the small opening that led down to the trail. As he hoisted himself inside, he could hear someone right behind him. Jeff took a few steps and forgot how steep it was when he thought he felt a hand glance at him in the darkness. He jumped and moved down the incline at a dangerous speed. He tried to find something to grab onto as his momentum was gaining.

He tried grabbing onto the vines along the wall that had helped him climb up, but he was moving too fast. The opening came up quickly as a blinding light as he fell onto the tree that he had climbed up earlier to get into the cave. Jeff bounced from one branch to another until he crashed into the far large limb. He was pretty sure his arm was broken, as he was powerless to stop himself from tumbling onto the tree. As his body hit the far large limb of the tree, Jeff looked down below to the 100-foot drop and there was nothing he could do as his body fell to the rocks below.

* * *

Freddy was more excited than ever after visiting the Casa Grande Ruins National Monument. He felt he had a better understanding of the history and the mystery of the Superstition Mountains. Freddy knew his sister was trying to figure out what happened at the cliff dwellings. He was torn between sharing with his sister what he had seen and giving his word to Naiche.

Was there a way to work around it? Keep his word yet share with his sister what he saw. He went back and forth, and the only solution was to take his sister there. Some time had passed, so Freddy was hoping she would be open to the hike. School was back in session, but it was still late summer and they would need to wait a few weeks to make that hike.

Freddy also replayed that day in his head over and over as he headed to the pool in the backyard. Would he be able to find the same spot he was taken to? He felt confident he would, but until he got there, he couldn't be sure. He wanted to go back. If his sister didn't want to go, he would find someone else.

Freddy floated on a raft in the pool, trying to come up with the right words. He wanted to go with his sister and show her firsthand. He felt he could keep his word to Naiche, not telling anyone. But if his sister saw what he did, he would be honest with both of them.

Sarah came out and cooled in the pool as well. At first, nothing was said as they both felt something had changed at the cliff dwellings last month.

Finally, Freddy felt he had nothing to lose. "You know, another few weeks and it will get cooler. Good hiking weather."

"In the mornings," Sarah replied, trying not to smile.

"Yep, the mornings. I sure would like to go on a hike with you again. Like we did in the Spring." Freddy said, trying to gauge his sister's interest.

"I guess I would be game for that. Nothing crazy though." Sarah answered, feeling good that she and her brother were having an actual conversation again.

"I know what your answer will be now. But think about it. I want to go back to the cliff dwelling. Back there with you." Freddy said as his eyes got larger.

"No frigging way," Sarah quickly answered.

"Well, think about it. That's all I'm asking. You keep asking me what happened up there. I can't tell you, but I want to show you. And you would have to keep it a secret."

Sarah listened to her brother. He had wanted to share something with her. She would need to think about it, but the more she thought, the more it sounded like she would go with her brother to the cliff dwellings.

* * *

Jose Rodriguez was coordinating a search and rescue with half a dozen volunteers on Cuff Button Trail. A group of horseback riders ran into a rattlesnake on the trail, which spooked the horse, sending its rider to the rocks.

At the time of the call, the rider was unconscious. Aurora 5 was in the far south part of the county and the other helicopter was helping in search of lost hikers near Roosevelt Lake. Jose and his team would get there to stabilize the injured rider and hope that one of the copters would get out to them soon.

By the time they got there, the rider was alert, but they had another issue, the rider's horse. The horse had a large cut on its front leg and seemed to be bleeding considerably. One of the other riders had taken a shirt to wrap the wound, but it wasn't helping much.

"Hello, I'm Deputy Rodriguez," Jose said to the group. "First things first, sir, how are you feeling?" Jose said, leaning over the rider who was seated in a small patch of shade against a rock.

"I'm okay. A little headache. Probably more embarrassed than anything." The gentleman answered.

"Sir, what's your name?"

"Chuck Granle." the man replied.

One volunteer started working on the man's cut, cleaning and dressing the wound. Jose radioed that a helicopter would be needed. Within a few minutes, Jose heard Austin Johnson's voice, "Copy that, we are on our way."

Another one of the volunteers walked over to Jose. "The horse is in bad shape. I'm not sure she can make it back. The leg doesn't look broken, but bleeding and a bad limp. Terry is on the radio with a vet clinic."

Jose looked at the horse and walked over to the group.

"This horse is in bad shape. Are one of you the owners?" Jose asked.

An older gentleman stepped forward, "Yes, I am."

"I'm not sure she can make it back to the trailhead. She is bleeding badly. We don't think it's broken, but probably not safe to have her walk back, at least now."

The older gentleman appeared a bit choked up. "I could stay the night with Betsy. Betsy is her name. See how it looks in the morning. This horse means the world to me."

"I've thought about that. A few of us can stay with the horse. I'm just not sure that is the best solution. She still may be just as bad tomorrow and lose more blood throughout the night." Jose said, looking over to Terry, who was on the radio with the vet.

"I'm open to anything. I'm not worried about the cost. Do you have a vehicle that can drive up here?"

"And carry a horse back? No. The only thing is a helicopter and we lifted her out." Jose said as Terry approached him.

"That's what the vet just told me. If we can get a harness made for the horse, get a copter to take her out." Terry explained.

"Terry, see if the helicopter has a harness for a full-size horse. If not, we need to find one." Jose said as he looked back at the horse.

Within a few minutes, Terry came back to the group. "Aurora 5 is picking up a harness. They'll be here within 30 minutes."

Jose turned to the group of riders. "Okay, we can airlift Betsy. We can airlift her to a vet clinic in Mesa. My thoughts are you riders head back. We'll get Chuck in a helicopter and depending on how he checks out, we'll probably get him to the hospital in Mesa."

The owner looked at Jose. "Should I stay as well to help Betsy?"

"It's your call, but we need to get the other horses and the riders back to the trailhead. Are any of these other horses yours?" Jose asked.

"Yes, all but one. Those are my trucks at the trailhead." He replied.

"Then I would get everyone else and the other horses back to the trailhead. Do you know where the clinic in Mesa is?" Jose asked.

"Yes, I do. It will take me some time to get over there," the owner said.

"Don't worry, we'll take care of Betsy. Talk to Terry and get the contact information of the vet. You can call them when you get the other horses taken care of," Jose said as he placed his hand on the gentleman's shoulder.

Within thirty minutes, the helicopter was circling above Jose and his team. They took Chuck to a flat clearing a few hundred feet where the helicopter could land. As they placed Chuck in the helicopter, a young woman got out of the helicopter with a harness.

"All right, I can't believe I'm saying this. This isn't the first time I've done this," she said as the group chuckled.

Within fifteen minutes, the horse was secured as they placed a blindfold on her, hoping it would help her not get spooked.

The helicopter slowly tightened the line and lifted the horse into the air. The horse appeared calm as Terry pulled out his cell phone and took a picture.

"I don't think I'll ever see this again," he said.

The young woman on the radio in the copter replied. "That's what I thought."

Jose and Terry watched the horse as it disappeared into the horizon.

The woman on the radio continued. "The tricky part is placing the horse down. You can't do it too fast or you'll break her leg."

"Well, Austin Johnson is the right pilot. I'm not sure if he ever did this before, but he's good, real good,"

Jose said as they gathered their things to get back to the trailhead.

14

In the late 1890s and early 1900s, Jim Bark held grazing rights on the south side of the Superstition Mountains. Today, numerous canyons and trails are named after him. Jim had always welcomed visitors to stay with him. One group was a geological survey team where they had found arrowheads. Later that year, residents of Mesa had come up to the mountains and uncovered over 100 arrowheads. They had stopped to show Jim their findings. Jim was more than happy to show them his collection of over 875 arrowheads![1]

* * *

If someone had told Sarah that she would be back at the cliff dwellings, she would have said they were nuts. They would have to start at the Woodbury Trailhead as her small truck couldn't handle the road to Rogers Trough, where Freddy and Lil had started their hike last month. Sarah and Freddy would need to go around the back way, which added some time to their hike.

Sarah wanted to make sure they had enough water, as she knew by midday the temperature would be close to 100 degrees. She knew it wasn't a good idea to go out this time of year, but they would take their time and stay hydrated. Sarah had told Jennifer they were headed to the cliff dwellings and worked out that Sarah would check in with Jennifer around 2:30 after Jennifer got off from work. Sarah told Jennifer if she didn't hear from her by 2:30, to call the authorities.

Sarah didn't want to be up there in the afternoon and hoped they could have a good pace in the morning and back to the truck way before the time she was to call Jennifer. Freddy had told her it would be a day she never forgot. She hoped it would be for all the right reasons.

So they started very early getting to the trailhead as the Sun was rising and the temperature was still comfortable. They had mapped out the trail and agreed to stop at regular intervals to drink. As time went on, Sarah forgot about their episode a few months back on the Woodbury Trail. She was getting caught up in her brother's adventure.

"Freddy, come on, can't you share with me what I'm going to see? Let me prepare." She said to her brother as they continued to hike up the canyon.

"I can't tell you. When we get there, you'll understand," Freddy said, turning back to his sister. "I promise."

It was another hour before they got to the cliff dwellings. They stopped in front and both sipped some water and then Freddy headed for the small room where Naiche had taken him through a hidden tunnel.

Freddy looked around, but something had changed. He wasn't sure what, but he couldn't find the opening.

"Freddy, what are we looking for?" Sarah asked.

"An opening. But I don't see it," Freddy said as he frantically looked around the room.

"Are you sure this is the right room?" Sarah asked.

"Yes, I'm almost positive," Freddy said as he looked at the large slap of stone in the back corner of the room.

"This wasn't here, last time, at least I don't remember it," as he tried to move it. "Sarah, help me."

Surprisingly, the two could slide the slap over a few feet. As the stone slid to the side, the opening that Freddy had gone through a few months back appeared.

Sarah turned to her brother. "We're going in there?"

"Yep, remember, this is a secret. You can't tell anyone about this," Freddy replied as he pulled out two flashlights from his backpack.

They both hoisted themselves up into the dark tunnel as Freddy shone the flashlight in front of him.

"You ready, sis? This will be fun," Freddy said with a large grin.

Sarah followed Freddy down the large tunnel. At first, Sarah was getting a little claustrophobic and couldn't help but wonder where her brother was leading her. He surely didn't want to talk about it with her, but he wanted her to see, firsthand, what he had seen.

The tunnel became larger to a point where finally they were both walking fully upright. It also appeared brighter, but Sarah wasn't sure if it was just her eyes becoming more acclimated in the darkness or if there was light coming in from somewhere.

Freddy turned back to his sister. "We're almost there."

Within a few minutes, Sarah could see light at the end of the tunnel. As they got closer to the end, she could see the light coming from around a corner.

"Now be quiet and stay down, just in case," Freddy said.

"In case of what?" Sarah asked.

"Hmm, I'm not sure. But just to be safe." Freddy and Sarah turned the corner and looked into the light.

He turned to his sister and stepped to the side so that she could get a good view. Sarah took a few steps forward and couldn't believe what she saw. A small community down below them, living in a cavern. Many openings throughout the cavern let in sunlight. Adrenalin rushed through her. There was so much to look at. So much so that she couldn't believe her eyes.

She turned to Freddy as he held his index finger up to his lips to remind her to be quiet. Sarah grabbed his hand and squeezed it tightly. They both squatted down and watched the community below. There were small fires on one side and she could smell they were cooking. Everyone seemed to be busy. She could make out some women weaving fabrics and another area where it appeared a small group of people were making tools from wood and stones.

Freddy whispered in her ear, "Naiche took me here."

"Who?" she asked.

"The boy who we saw with the snake on Woodbury Trail. He lives here. He says we must keep this a secret. I promised him I would," Freddy said.

"You know what? No one would believe us anyway." She smirked with excitement.

The two stayed and watched for another thirty minutes before they headed back. Sarah took a few pictures with her cell phone, making sure the flash was off. Then they slowly went back down the tunnel to which they came. They both had thoughts filling their heads. What they had seen. How many others knew of this community and what did it mean? How long was it there? Sarah now understood why her brother became so interested in Native American history over the last month.

They finally made it back to the cliff dwelling. As they made their way out of the tunnel into the small room and then slid the large flat rock over the opening. They turned to each other, both with big grins. Sarah looked at the time on her phone. Later than she planned, but should be back at their truck by 2:30. As they headed back down the trail to the truck. Sarah turned to her brother.

"Oh, my God. Freddy, this is incredible! Thank you." She said as she skipped along the trail.

* * *

Lil had been at the trailheads before 6 am when she knew she would see a majority of the hikers head out. Although she was up early, she was rewarded by finishing up by noon. She had some time finally to catch up on some errands. Lil knew she was low on groceries, so she headed to the store on the way home. She picked up the typical essentials, eggs, milk, some bread, and a few bottles of wine.

The store seemed unusually busy, although this wasn't the typical day and time she would go to the grocery store. She glanced at the lines and the self-checkout and they seemed incredibly long, so she waited in one of the shorter checkouts which had a cashier.

She finally got her items on the conveyor belt and was getting her credit card out when the cashier spoke.

"Ranger Shanta? From the Superstitions?" the young girl cashier said.

"It's Jennifer. We've met a few times," Jennifer said.

"Oh yes. You just caught me off guard. I didn't put the two together. I didn't know you worked here?" Lil said with a smile.

"Yes, for a few months now. I usually have to work on the weekend, but what are you going to do? Probably good, nothing for me to do today. Sarah and Freddy are going back to the cliff dwellings and that's too long a hike for me."

Lil's smile disappeared. "Oh, back to the dwellings? I thought Sarah didn't want to go back there," Lil inquired.

I guess Freddy now says he wants to show her something," Jennifer said as she started scanning Lil's purchases. "They are calling me later to make sure everything is okay." Jennifer continued.

"When did they leave? It's still pretty hot out there this time of year." Lil asked as she quickly placed her credit card in the reader.

"Early this morning. Like I said, Sarah said she would call me around 2:30 when I get out of work. Just to make sure everything is okay. If I don't hear from her, she told me to call someone. Actually, I'm not sure who to call," Jennifer said as she continued to complete the sale.

Lil looked at her watch. It was a little after one. "No need to call anyone. I'm actually headed there now. I'll look for them." Lil said as she quickly grabbed her bag and left the store.

On her way to her truck, she threw her groceries into a garbage can and got into her pickup, and sped down Route 60 to Rogers Trough Trailhead.

* * *

Sarah and Freddy were still making their way back to Woodbury Trailhead. Although their route was longer than the traditional route, they were both so excited and discussing what they had seen that it seemed to go quickly.

"Sarah, please tell me you won't tell anyone," Freddy pleaded.

"Yeah, okay, it's just so incredible," she said, wanting to believe her words.

She felt her phone vibrate in her pocket so she knew she finally had cell coverage. She pulled out her phone to check the time, 1:40 PM.

"Freddy, remind me to call Jennifer in another half hour," Sarah said.

"You cannot tell Jennifer. She can't keep a secret." Freddy said, as his voice got more excited.

"I know, I know. I just told her we were going on a hike back to the cliff dwellings. With this heat and being more remote than some other hikes, I told her if I didn't call her when she gets off work to send someone to look for us."

"Damn, I'm glad we are headed back. We can't let anyone know about this. You promised," Freddy said as he picked up the pace.

It was almost a half hour and the two stopped to drink some water and dialed Jennifer. There was no answer, so she left a message.

"Jen, It's me, Sarah. Freddy and I are headed back to my pickup. Everything is good. Thanks."

A minute went by and Sarah's phone rang. It was Jennifer.

"Hey Jen, did you get my message?" Sarah asked her.

"I did. By the way, Ranger Shanta was in the store. I kind of told her you two were at the cliff dwellings." Jennifer said.

"Why did you tell her that?"

"It just kind of came out. She said she was headed there anyway, so she'll look for you." Jennifer explained.

"Okay. Thanks for letting me know. I'll call you later." Sarah said as she put her phone away.

Sarah turned to Freddy. "Jennifer ran into Ranger Shanta and told her we were up here."

"See, you can't tell Jennifer anything. I hope we don't run into her, at least not right now," Freddy said.

"Yeah, me either. I don't have a poker face like you. If we hustle, I'm sure we can get out of here before she gets here." Sarah said as they both picked up their pace.

* * *

Lil was racing down the primitive road, faster than her truck could handle comfortably, but she wanted to get to the cliff dwelling as soon as possible. Her mind was racing. What were those two kids up to? The cliff dwellings had become a dangerous place and too much of a focus lately. She didn't want anything to add to it.

She knew from what Jennifer told her she would be cutting it close and could very easily have missed them. But if they found something, they would get caught up in it and probably still be there. In this heat, they may also be exhausted and dehydrated on the trail. She finally arrived at Rogers Trough. A few cars in the parking lot. Maybe she wasn't too late. She placed two large water containers in her backpack and started up the trail. She could see numerous fresh footprints on the trail. By the time she reached the trail where it met up with the Reavis Valley Trail, the prints on the path no longer seemed fresh. Did the kids actually come out? Maybe they figured it was too hot? Maybe they started at the Woodbury Trailhead.

At this point, she would go to the dwelling and see if they were still there or traces that they may have been there. In another two miles, she would have her answer. She just had a bad feeling.

* * *

Sarah and Freddy were exhausted as they approached Sarah's truck in the Woodbury trailhead parking lot.

"So far, so good," Freddy said as he scanned the parking lot.

"Maybe we're going to pass her on the way out on the dirt road," Sarah replied, still thinking about Ranger Shanta.

"Could be, but she might not know what your pickup looks like. Put your hair up in your hat and here wear my sunglasses. If we see a car coming, I'll duck." Freddy said as he handed his sister his sunglasses.

The two drove down the dirt road for what felt like an eternity for them. They talked about what they had seen and planned on going back to the Casa Grande Ruin. This time, Sarah would be more engaged.

As they were approaching Route 60 another pickup truck was headed their way. Sarah and Freddy's smiles faded quickly as Freddy ducked out of sight and Sarah placed her left hand on her chin as they made their way past the oncoming truck. It was a false alarm, just looked like more hikers. Freddy sat back up in the seat as Sarah's truck turned down Route 60.

"Remember, this is all a secret," Freddy said seriously.

"I know, I know, but can we really keep this a secret? Should we? Maybe we should talk to someone?"

"Who, Mom and Dad? They'll never let us hike again. Ranger Shanta? I like her, but you don't seem to?" Freddy replied.

"I guess she is okay. I just think we need time to think about telling anyone about it. That's why I didn't want to run into her. What about Deputy Ligai? He seemed nice." Sarah answered.

"I don't know. I thought we were going to keep this a secret." Freddy said with a bit of disgust in his tone.

"I won't say anything to anyone unless we both agree, okay?" Sarah said, calming her brother down.

* * *

Lil made it to the cliff dwellings. She had gone through more water than expected, but in this heat, she knew she needed to stay hydrated. Lil did a quick glance throughout the dwellings for Sarah and Freddy or anyone. She noticed fresh footprints in the dust.

"Sarah, Freddy. Are you here?" Lil called out a few times but got no answer.

Lil focused on the footprints and noticed they led to a small room in the back of the dwelling. The prints headed to the back corner of the room and seemed to end there. It didn't make much sense. Lil got down on her knee to look closer at the prints. They led right to the wall.

Lil noticed a large slab against the wall and she saw that there was a mark on the floor like the slab was slid over and then back. She leveraged her weight and pushed it to the side. At first, it barely moved, but once she found the right angle, she could move it. There in front of her was an opening, a tunnel. She pulled out a flashlight from her backpack. Is this where the kids went to? If not the kids, someone was in here recently. Were they still in there? Only one way to find out. Lil hoisted herself up into the tunnel. She turned on her flashlight and moved onward. Only one way to get some answers, she thought.

15

Throughout the 1950s, over a dozen accounts were reported of people gone missing in the Superstition Mountains. The bodies were eventually found. Many of them were found with bullet holes in their heads.[1]

* * *

The next morning, two hikers came across a body on Pinto Peak. A call came from the sheriff's dispatch and Cal was on his way. The body they had found last month still turned up as a Jane Doe. Was this body at Pinto's Peak one of the three Cal was looking for?

Once the area was examined, they would call in a helicopter to take the body away. Jose was on his way to Pinto Peak, as he was out in the area already. Cal would go out with the helicopter if another call didn't come in. He was hoping to have dinner with Lil tonight, although she hadn't gotten back to him on his text this morning.

Within the hour, Cal was at the airfield and headed to Pinto Peak. Cal knew Jose had just got to the site and was doing some preliminary assessment on the scene. As the helicopter landed, Cal made his way to Jose.

"So, what do we have here?" Cal said, looking over Jose's shoulder to see where the body lay.

"41-year-old Caucasian male. Jeff Albright from Salt Lake City. Looks like a massive blow to the head," Jose said as he turned and walked with Cal to the body, "but no blood where he laid, nothing on his clothes, nothing here. I don't think he died here."

"What about tracks, anything?" Cal inquired.

"That's the other thing. Nothing. Say he fell a quarter mile from here, then collapsed. From what direction? The only prints you see around here are the two hikers who went off the trail a bit and mine. There should be something." Jose said.

"We can scan the area in a few directions. If he fell around here, we should find a site with some blood." Cal said as he looked at the ground around the body.

"A forensic team is going to be radioing in with a few directions. I know they're already talking about specific pictures and videos. I've done this with them once before." Jose said as he laid down some markers near the body.

It was a good few hours before Jose and Cal recorded as much information as they could and combed the area to see if there were any signs of him coming from one direction versus another.

As they placed the body of Jeff Albright into the helicopter, Cal turned to Jose. "So I'm sure you've been thinking the same thing I am. If the trauma to his head was done somewhere else, he's at least 180 pounds and his body was dumped here, someone did a good job of cleaning up any traces."

"Yep, I'm thinking that. Maybe when they do an autopsy, they'll have some ideas. I have a feeling we may be out here later this week." Jose said as he gave the thumbs up to the pilot.

Jose and Cal were downloading the pictures and videos from earlier into the computer and sending them off to the forensic lab.

"Cal, do you want to grab some dinner when our shift is over?" Jose said as he was attaching some data to the server.

Cal looked at his cell phone. He had texted Lil a second time earlier and still had no reply. "Sure, sounds good," he said.

* * *

Sarah and Freddy's heads were still spinning on what they had seen the day before. What did it mean? Who else knows about this? Sarah felt they should tell someone and Freddy remained adamant that it should remain a secret.

They had stayed up late sitting in their backyard at the fire pit. Almost as soon as Freddy's head hit this pillow, he was asleep. Sarah, however, lay in bed for hours. She couldn't turn her mind off.

She tossed and turned and she kept glancing at the small digital clock next to her bed. There was a full moon and she had her curtains open so she could see the moon and stars. It was 2:12 as she glanced once again at the clock. She closed her eyes. She figured if she could fall asleep in the next few minutes, she could still get six hours of sleep.

Sarah opened her eyes as she thought she heard something outside in the yard. She turned to the window and sure enough, she saw a shadow race past her window. Sarah thought now her mind was playing tricks on her. She would never fall asleep. Then she heard another sound, like a window being jimmied open. She got out of her bed and she could see a figure outside of her brother's bedroom window trying to open the window.

"Freddy!" Sarah screamed instinctively.

The figure turned towards Sarah. As he moved away from Freddy's window and took a step forward, the moonlight made his features clearer. He looked like one of the men they had seen in the Superstition Mountains.

Sarah screamed again, "Freddy" and this time the light from Freddy's room came on as well as lights throughout the house. Sarah could hear her parents running through the house.

The figure looked at Sarah and then dashed to the far back of the yard and jumped over the fence as Sarah's father entered her room.

"Are you okay, honey?" Sarah's father said as Freddy came running into Sarah's room along with their mother.

"There was someone in the yard. They were trying to break into Freddy's window." She said, looking at Freddy.

"I'll call the police," their mother said as she raced into the kitchen to call 911.

Within ten minutes, two squad cars were parked outside. One officer looked in the backyard as another officer asked Sarah what she had seen.

"It was too dark to get a good look. All I can tell you is it was a man." Sarah said.

The other officer walked into the house. "I don't see anything."

The officer who had been speaking with Sarah turned to their parents. "We'll circle the area a few times tonight. I don't think they'll be back, but if so, we'll get them," the officer said with confidence.

Sarah's father shook hands. "Thank you, officers," as he walked them to the door.

Their mother turned to Freddy and Sarah, "Go back to bed. Your father and I will probably be up the rest of the night and like the officer said, they'll be patrolling in the area. Nothing to worry about."

Sarah knew more than she shared with the officers. Tomorrow, she would share it with Freddy. Something had to be done or the mysterious figure in front of Freddy's window would be back.

The following morning, Sarah pulled out the business card that Cal had given her when they were all at the cliff dwellings. She had arranged for them all to meet in the parking lot at the Hieroglyphic Trailhead at 10 am.

It was still summer and most hikers would be on their way back at that time and they would have some privacy. She wasn't even sure where to start and if Deputy Ligai would believe them. Freddy was still upset that they were breaking his promise to Naiche, but after what his sister saw, he knew she was right to reach out to someone. They both trusted Deputy Ligai, so he seemed like a logical person.

Cal was waiting for the two when Sarah's old pickup pulled into the lot. Even though there was a spot near the front of the trailhead, she drove to the back, where there weren't any vehicles. Sarah and Freddy got out of their truck and waved to Cal.

He noticed they weren't walking to the gate, so he walked to them. As he approached them, he could tell they were nervous.

"Hey, guys, what's up?" Cal said with a big smile.

Sarah looked up at Cal and then her eyes went down. "We have something to share with you that you won't believe. Nobody will."

"Okay, I'll have an open mind, I promise," Cal said, holding his smile, trying to relax the kids.

"It's about the cliff dwellings we were all at," Sarah said.

"I didn't get lost," Freddy chimed in and continued. "When Ranger Shanta and I were there, I met a boy a few years older than me. Well, we met him on the Woodbury Trail a few months earlier when he saved Sarah from the snake."

"And Freddy thinks he's seen him a few times when we've hiked," Sarah added.

"Okay. Did Ranger Shanta meet this boy?" Cal asked.

"No, she never saw him. When she was on the radio, he came out of nowhere. Well, really not of nowhere, a hidden tunnel. He took me in the tunnel." Freddy said.

"So you found a hidden tunnel and went in it with this boy in the cliff dwellings. You realize there are many mines left by prospectors as well as caves created by air pockets and lava tubes," Cal said, still perplexed at their faces.

"It's not the tunnel really what we're here to talk about. It's about what's at the end of it." Freddy said.

Immediately, Cal thought they had found a skeleton, or they found a mine that had gold.

Cal squatted down to get lower and looked up at the two. "Did you find a body?", no answer. "Did you find gold?" Cal chuckled.

"No," Sarah said. "Freddy saw a small village in a cave, with over a hundred people living there."

"Freddy, are you sure? Are you sure this wasn't a dream you had? Some dreams seem real. You didn't say anything when we found you a few months back," Cal replied.

"It wasn't a dream. I didn't say anything because I promised Naiche I wouldn't." Freddy said.

"Who is Naiche?" Cal asked.

"It's the boy that lives there. He showed me his home. He asked me not to tell anyone." Freddy said.

"Freddy, people have been searching these mountains for hundreds of years looking for gold. If people were living in caves, someone would have found them a long time ago." Cal said as he stood up.

"I wouldn't have believed him either. But he took me there two days ago. I saw it too. It's real," Sarah said as she started getting excited.

"Did you tell your parents? What did they say?" Cal asked.

"No, Freddy wanted to keep his secret, but after last night it's not safe," Sarah said as her eyes watered up.

"What happened last night?" Cal asked.

"Someone tried to break into Freddy's room in the middle of the night. I saw them. It was one of the men from that cave. He ran off when I screamed." Sarah said.

"Yeah, and the police came, but he was gone by then," Freddy said.

Cal looked at the two as they were almost trembling. "If it was anyone else, I know I wouldn't believe them. But you're good kids. I'll go take a look at this tunnel and cave, but if you're lying, fabricating this story, you will be in a lot of trouble."

"Take a look at these," Sarah said as she showed him photos from her cell phone. "I know they're dark, but you can see them. It's real."

Cal looked at the photos. They were dark, but they looked like people in an adobe village. "You said they were Native Americans. How do you know? Maybe they were another group of people," Cal said, still looking at the pictures.

"Naiche and the people below were dressed like the Native American wardrobes we've seen," Sarah said.

Freddy quickly added, "They were dark skin. A little like you."

"Can you tell me exactly where this tunnel is?" Cal asked.

"We can take you there," Freddy said.

You know what. I'm not sure what you saw, exactly. So it's safer for you to stay here. Frankly, until I take a look, I'm not going to bring anyone up there. I'm not sure if it's just some squatters or what." Cal explained.

"It's the back wall of a small room if the complex of the dwellings. Right Freddy," Sarah said.

"Yeah. Slide that slate over and get up there. At first, you can only crawl, but then you can eventually stand. In about twenty minutes, you come to a turn where the buildings are below you and you can look down."

"Okay. And you're sure one of those people was at your home last night trying to break in? Maybe it was one of your friends."

"It was dark last night, but he had the same clothes as the people in that cave," Sarah said.

"All right, I'll go check this out.   I'll call you later.   Stay away from there for now, promise?" Cal said as a smile returned to his face.

"We are staying out of the Superstitions for a while," Sarah said, feeling better after sharing their experience with Cal.

Cal left the kids and headed to Rogers Trough.   On one hand, if the kids were correct in what they saw, this would be significant, and will need help in this situation.   On the other hand, if is something different, there would be no need to get others involved. The first thing was to call Jose and make sure he wasn't already tied up if something came up.

Cal drove south on Route 60 and dialed Jose. "Jose, it's Cal.   I'm headed to Rogers Trough to check on something. Nothing important, but I wanted to check on your status."

"Brother sounds like you love that place. You keep ending up there. I'm good right now. I know we have most of the volunteers available." Jose answered.

"Great.   Like I said, nothing urgent, but I want to check something and get it off my plate." Cal said as he was making his way out of Gold Canyon.

"Cal, not sure if you saw it yet. It looks like we have a name for our Jane Doe from the Woodbury Trail. It's a Sandee Davenport. Sandee with two E's, not a Y." Jose told him.

"I hadn't heard. Well, I told you about Waylen telling me about a Sandy Davenport. It still took a long time to figure it out." Cal said as he continued down the 60.

"The dental records were a match with a Sandee Orlinski from Chicago. She had gotten married and became a Davenport shortly before she went missing." Jose replied.

"It's good we finally have a name. I'll look it over when I get into the office." Cal said.

"Yep. Hope you find what you're looking for," Jose said.

"Me too, thanks," Cal said as he hung up, not sure what he wanted to find.

The drive up the primitive road seemed longer today. He knew he still had a long hike followed by twenty-plus minutes through a tunnel that Freddy and Sarah had told him about. He drove on thinking there were so many unanswered issues, nothing would surprise him.

Still three unanswered disappearances. Two of them, someone impersonating Pinal officials, were reaching out to the family. Who would do this and why?

Cal pulled up to the trailhead and made sure he had enough water with him and that his flashlight had fresh batteries. Hiking up the trail by himself, he took it at a much quicker pace than normal. First, he didn't want Jose to get caught short-handed, and second, he wanted to see if there was anything to what the kids had seen.

He finally arrived at the cliff dwelling. It didn't take him long to find the room the kids had told him about. Sure enough, the far corner had a large flat stone that, although it could easily be overlooked, appeared as though it was slid to the side. Sure enough, as Cal pushed it to the side, a hole appeared in the wall.

Cal hoisted himself up and started doing a crab walk for the first thirty feet until he could straighten out a bit. It was still another 50 feet until he could stand up. Cal kept going and looking for a light towards the back of the tunnel the kids had spoken of but nothing yet.

Cal kept the light from the flashlight ahead of him so that he didn't hit his head and twist his ankle in a hole. He eventually came to what looked like what might be the end of the tunnel. As it got a little brighter, Cal could see the tunnel walls now without his flashlight.

Sure enough, in the end, there was a turn to the left with a large opening. The opening expanded into a large cavern just as the kids had said, except there were no people. He could see the building below, but he had no idea how old they might be.

Cal took his flashlight to search for a path down to the buildings below. Within a few minutes, Cal was on the floor of the cavern. From the bottom floor, the cavern appeared even larger. There were several openings along the wall above that let in natural light.

He searched throughout the structures, trying to gauge what the kids may have seen. There didn't appear to be any footprints on the floor. He ran his finger along the soot over what appeared to be ovens. His finger turned dark black, fresh soot.

He continued to examine the area, looking for traces to collaborate on what the kids had seen. The structure appeared sturdy and didn't seem brittle like the dwellings in which he entered. He went back to the ovens and he found remnants of what looked like prickly pear cactus.

In another room, he found a broken bowl, but again too difficult to determine the age. He took pictures with his camera and although part of him told him not to disturb what could be artifacts, and placed the bowl in his backpack.

As he made his way back up to the opening from which he came, he saw the familiar drawing that he had been seeing over the last six months. Multiple warriors or hunters with longhorn sheep. The sun lay above all of them, but higher up was a large white warrior looking down on them. It was much bigger than the other drawing he had encountered.

He made his way to the entrance and looked again, trying to remember the photo the kids had shown him. He took a few photos and then headed back up the tunnel to get back to the cliff dwelling.

The time seemed to go by quickly and he was soon in the small room, sliding back the rock to cover the opening. He did a quick check of his cell, but he still had no service and the radio seemed quiet. He headed back to the trailhead, wondering what his next move should be.

As he turned out of the dwellings, he saw Lil on the radio, standing there on the ridge.

"Are you looking for me?" Cal said as Lil turned as Cal had startled her.

"Hmm, I didn't hear you," she said.

"Did Jose tell you I was up here?" he said as he wiped the dust off his clothes.

"Yeah, I ran into him and he told me you were up here." She said as she put away her radio.

"Looks like you've been busy," as she pointed to his dirty clothes.

"Lil, there is a cavern behind these walls," Cal turned and then continued. "The two kids, Sarah and Freddy, came across a tunnel. They came to me with this story that there was a village in the cavern."

"So you came up here to check it out. What did you find?" she asked Cal as she wiped more dust off his shirt.

"There is some type of village or remains of one. Do you want to see it?" Cal said, noticing all the dust on Lil.

"I've seen it Cal. It's abandoned." Lil replied.

"I would agree, but they showed me photos," Cal said.

"I don't think they were of this ruin," Lil said.

"Either way, what we just saw is new, right? I've never heard of this village." Cal said as he pulled out water to drink.

"Yes, it is new. Cal, let me take care of this. It falls within the Tonto Forest. Can you keep this quiet for a while? If it gets out, we're going to have every gold hunter and looter going through the cavern before we can properly determine what we are looking at."

"Of course. Should we do anything now or head back?" Cal replied.

"Let's head back. I'll work with my boss on how he wants to handle this. Just please don't tell anyone. No one can keep a secret." Lil said as the two headed back to the trailhead.

The Sun was settling in the west by the time they got to the parking lot.

"Where's your pickup, Lil?" Cal asked.

"Oh, it's parked just a bit behind the lot down the road," Lil said, pointing to the truck behind a large bush.

"Did you want to grab any dinner or drinks? I tried to leave you a message yesterday but didn't hear back."

"I'm sorry, it was a crazy day yesterday and well, I'm beat. I'll take a rain check," she said with a smile.

The two made their way down the primitive road back to Route 60. Cal was still trying to put together the story the kids told him and what he saw. Lil had seen the cavern and felt it was abandoned. She probably knew best. He would talk to the kids tomorrow after sleeping on it.

16

In October 1960, hikers found a headless skeleton in the Superstition Mountains. Seventy feet away, they found his skull with two bullet holes in it. The remains were eventually identified as Franz Harrier, a student from Australia.[1]

* * *

The next morning Cal texted Sarah and asked her and Freddy to meet him at the Gold Canyon Sheriff's station. He also said it might be a good idea to bring her parents. Cal sat in the small conference room in the back. He had thought about it all night. The two logical explanations for this were the kids were playing a hoax or they had stumbled across another cavern beside the one Cal was in. He didn't think either was the answer. He could sense that Sarah and Freddy were good kids and he couldn't imagine two caverns containing structures in the same area. The kids gave good directions and they led him to the exact spot of the tunnel.

The door from the conference room was open and he could see the kids entering the building. Cal was disappointed that they didn't bring their parents, but if that point came, he would go visit them.

Sarah and Freddy were escorted into the conference room as Cal extended his hand to one side of the table.

"Guys, thanks for coming in. I see your parents aren't here. Are they coming later?" Cal asked.

"No. We wanted to hear what you found. See if you thought the people in the cavern might be the ones in our yard," Sarah replied.

"I went to the cavern. It was empty of people, that is. Are you sure you didn't get scared the other night when someone was trying to break into your house and your imaginations took over," Cal said calmly.

Freddy jumped to his feet. "No, no, I saw the cavern twice. Both times there were maybe a hundred people."

"Not sure there were a hundred, but we saw a lot of people," Sarah added.

"I went in the tunnel but not a sole there. I went down to the floor and nothing. Well, except for an old bowl, but probably there for a hundred years. Ranger Shanta went to see it too, and she didn't see anyone. She feels it's been vacant for a very long time." Cal said as he wanted to calm the kids down.

"What about the pictures I showed you?" Sarah asked.

"Can I see those again?" Cal pulled out his cell phone and went to the photos. "Let's see. Let's compare them."

Cal was stunned. They surely looked like the same place. The structures, the walls, they all appeared to be identical.

"See, the same," Freddy said.

"Yes, except the people," Cal said, more confused than last night.

"I think they saw us and that's why they tried to break into Freddy's room the other night," Sarah said.

"I don't know about that. Could be just a coincidence, and your minds are getting the best of you." Cal said as he put his phone away. "Sarah, can you text me your photos?"

"Sure thing," she replied.

"Okay. I'm not sure what's going on. The first thing is don't share this with any friends, no one except your parents. Ranger Shanta is talking to her boss who runs the Tonto Forest and they'll take a closer look at the cavern. She is worried about looters if people find out until it can be examined." Cal said to the kids.

"Okay, no one will believe us anyway," Sarah said.

"Right," Cal answered quickly. "I'm going to check with the Apache Junction Police and make sure they keep an eye on your house for the next few nights."

"Thanks," Freddy acknowledged as he got up.

"Sit tight. We'll find out what's going on," Cal said as he walked the kids to the door.

Before he got back to the desk, his cell phone chirped. Three photos from Sarah. He looked at that again. It was unsettling, as they looked to be in the same place. He called the sheriff's office and asked for forensics.

"Can I send you a few photos and can you tell if they've been photoshopped at all?" Cal asked, knowing they could.

"Thanks, I'll be sending them over in a few minutes," he said as he then quickly dialed Lil, but there was no answer.

The morning went by quickly and Cal's shift ended mid-afternoon, as he had started early. After speaking with the kids this morning, he was still at a loss for what was going on. He figured he would take the broken bowl he found to the Tonto National Forest Office in Phoenix. With everything that was going on, he had forgotten he had it in his backpack.

Traffic was lite and he was there within a half hour. When he entered, he introduced himself and asked to speak with the Supervisor. A few minutes later, he was escorted into Supervisor Gannet. An older gentleman who held the position for many years.

"What can I do for you Deputy Ligai?" he said he a deep husky voice.

I realize Ranger Shanta probably told you about the cavern we found. It's really something, " Cal continued as he pulled out the broken bowl from his backpack, "I realize I should have left this there. Anyway, is there any way you can tell the age of this?"

Supervisor Gannet seemed a bit irritated. "No, you shouldn't have taken that," as he reached for it as Cal handed it over. "I'm not sure what cavern you're talking about, but I can tell you this bowl is maybe a few years old. Very nice work, but not an artifact. Where did you say you got this?"

Cal reached back for it," The cavern near the Cliff Dwelling in Rogers Canyon that Ranger Shanta told you about."

"She hasn't said anything to me. There are a lot of caverns there, but probably nothing to get excited about. Was that all you wanted, to see how old the bowl was?" the Supervisor sat back down in his chair.

"That's it. I guess I thought it might be a lot older. I'm sorry to have wasted your time," Cal said.

"Not wasting anyone's time. Stop in anytime." The supervisor said as he quickly got up again to shake Cal's hand and then sat down.

Cal left Phoenix and headed back to the Pinal Sheriff's Office. He was getting frustrated as he was not getting any answers, just more questions.

His phone rang as he turned down the 202, "Deputy Ligai,"

"Cal, it's Brenda from the forensic team. I just wanted to let you know about the pictures you sent us."

"Yes, that was quick," Cal said.

"Well, because it was pretty straightforward. No enhancements or photoshopped on the picture. It's clean. Hope that helps."

"Thanks." although Cal wasn't sure if it helped or just added to everything going on.

Cal met up with Jose at the Peralta Trailhead, as he knew he was helping an injured hiker earlier in the morning.

"Jose, I'm glad you're still here. I know I've thrown a lot of crazy shit at you since I joined the team, but this is beyond crazy."

Jose chuckled at Cal. "Alright brother, let's hear it."

"The kids from the Cliff Dwelling in Roger Canyon," Cal began.

"Yes, I remember you told me about them. They seemed like good kids, you said. Are they okay?" Jose asked.

"Yes, but someone tried to break into the boys' room the other night."

"Oh wow, but you said they're fine. Did they find out who?" Jose said in a more concerned tone.

"No, but the kids came to me with who they thought it might be. It has to do with when we were looking for Freddy. He claimed he actually found, I guess you would call it, a hidden village in a cavern." Cal said.

"Another ruin? The Superstitions are filled with them. That's exciting for him but I don't follow on how that has anything to do with someone trying to break in. Did he take some artifacts? Some of those are pretty valuable." Jose inquired.

"He didn't take anything, but what he saw was a group of people living in there. He eventually told Sarah his sister. They went there again a few days and she said she saw the same thing. So they think someone saw them and that's why they were trying to break into their home the other night." Cal continued as the two walked to Jose's truck.

"Sounds like some squatters. We should check it out. Get some more people involved, probably the Tonto Forest Officials as well." Jose said.

"The kids thought they were Native Americans, but anyway, as I told you yesterday, I went to check it out and there was no one there. I found the cavern. Saw the building and structures but it was abandoned. Lil had caught up with me. She said you had told her I was headed there. She said she thought it was abandoned for some time." Cal said.

"I'm confused. I didn't talk to Lil yesterday, and it sounds like the kids either are pulling your legs or they were at a different location." Jose said.

"I thought the same thing," Cal said as he pulled out his cell phone. "I talked to the kids again this morning and Sarah had taken a picture. Here, this one," Cal said as he showed Jose his cell phone. "And this one is the one I took the next day. Just about the same location. You can see it's the same place. I checked. The photo wasn't doctored up."

Jose looked at both photos a few times. "Okay, it is kind of weird. I think we need to get some more people involved, though."

"Lil said she would be talking to her supervisor about it and there is no one there anymore, so not much to do. Lil asked me not to tell anyone until the Tonto

Forest decides on how to handle it if it is a ruin. They don't want a swarm of people right away," Cal said.

"That makes sense. Can you tell me where it is? I have the day off tomorrow and would love to check it out." Jose asked.

"Of course," Cal continued to share with him the location. "Jose, let me know what you think. I'm still not sure it's an abandoned ruin," Cal said as he headed to his truck and then turned to Jose. "And you said you didn't speak with Lil yesterday?"

"No, not me. Maybe someone else you told. Actually, I didn't mention it to anyone." Jose replied.

"Thanks. It must have been someone else," Cal said, knowing he didn't share it with anyone but Jose.

Cal went back to the office and tried to make sense of everything. At least three people over the last dozen years were originally called missing in the Superstitions. In those three searches, a second call came in from a family member that they were returned home and the search was called off. The families were all contacted by someone claiming to be in law enforcement, and they were still actively searching for their family members.

A fourth missing person's remains, Sandy Davenport, were found. She also at one time had a search in the Superstitions and they were called off. Maybe it came with the job, but it seemed to be all falling in his lap.

He pulled out his cell and sent a text to Lil. "I need to see you tonight."

"Why don't you come over around 6:30 PM? I'll make dinner," Lil's text answered.

Cal gathered a few items to take home with him, as although he had a few days off, he knew he would be looking for answers. He made his way to Lil's home in Apache Junction. The sun was setting on the Superstitions and it took on a pink glow. The majestic view never grew old.

Cal pulled into Lil's driveway. He wasn't expecting someone like Lil. They had so much in common and seemed to have an instant chemistry. She had so much knowledge and insight on the Superstition Mountains. She also had some mystery. But as he was feeling closer to her, he also felt there was something off. It was nothing he could put his finger on. Maybe it was just his imagination with everything going on. He was never good in relationships and it could be just that simple.

Lil had made one of her Native American dishes that Cal enjoyed. Cal shared what he had learned about the body of Sandee Davenport. Lil shared with Cal about a couple of hikers she had found that had a campfire. They spoke about everything except what was on their minds, the cavern the kids found.

Lil was in the kitchen drying the last of the plates from dinner as Cal poured two drinks and placed one on the counter next to Lil.

"We need to talk," Cal said, looking into Lil's eyes.

"What do you want to talk about?" Lil asked as she took her drink and walked over to the kitchen table and took a seat.

"Really? Let's start with the cavern the kids came across," Cal said with frustration.

"What about it? I spoke to my boss Doug Gannet first thing this morning. He agreed with me to keep quiet until we can go through it thoroughly." Lil said.

"You spoke to him this morning?" Cal asked.

"Yes. First thing. I think it was 8 am," Lil replied.

Cal's head leaned to the side. "I guess it was good you ran into Jose yesterday so you could find me."

"He told me you were headed there and I was headed to the trailhead, anyway," Lil replied, wondering where Cal was headed in his questioning.

"And you had seen the cavern prior to me. How did you find it?"

"I just started thinking about when we couldn't find Freddy last month. I started looking and then I found the entrance. Cal, why all the questions? What are you getting at?" Lil asked.

"I'm looking for the truth," Cal said, taking a sip of his drink. "There's more to that cavern than you're telling me. Do you want to share anything with me? Lil, I've grown very attached to you, but I need honesty."

"So you think I'm not being honest with you?" Lil asked.

"I know you're not. First, Jose said he didn't talk to you yesterday." Cal said.

"Maybe it was someone else. I thought it was Jose." Lil quickly said.

"He was the only one who knew. Also, I went to see your boss today. He had no idea about the cavern." Cal went on as Lil looked solemnly at him. "The kids showed me a picture they took the day before. Same cavern and there were people there."

"Cal," Lil reached out to hold his hand. "There is a good reason I haven't been hundred percent upfront with you. It hurts me because I have strong feelings for you."

"Well, I'd love to hear your reason," Cal replied.

"It's not an easy thing to explain. I think it will be easier to show you," Lil said.

"Show me?" Cal asked.

"Yes. Tomorrow, in the Superstitions." Lil said as she squeezed Cal's hand.

"Just tell me," Cal said as he pulled his hand away.

"I can't. It's something I need to show you." Lil said, feeling the pain Cal was sharing.

"Okay, where, what time?" Cal asked as he stood from the table.

"We can leave first thing in the morning," Lil said.

"I'm going home tonight. Tell me where we should meet." Cal said as he pulled out his car keys from his pocket.

"7 am, at Tortilla. Where we took our first hike together."

"I'll see you then," Cal said as he opened the front door.

"Cal, don't be mad. There is a good reason for all of this. You will see tomorrow. Please understand, I didn't want to keep anything from you. After tomorrow, there will be no secrets."

Cal opened the door and left.

* * *

The following morning, Cal drove down Route 88 to Tortilla. He tossed most of the night, trying to put the puzzle together. What was Lil going to show him? Why couldn't she explain it to him? What were the secrets and what was she hiding?

As Cal approached the trailhead, he saw Lil's truck at the far side of the parking lot. He pulled next to her and grabbed his backpack and water from the back of the car.

Lil walked up to Cal, "Good morning. I think shortly you'll understand everything."

Cal nodded and turned towards the trail. "This way I assume."

"Actually no. Follow me," Lil said as she headed east in an unmarked clearing.

Not much was said as they climbed up the mountain that flanked Fish Creek Canyon. Eventually, they were in the narrow canyon for a short time. Lil then left the canyon for a small narrow path that would take them up Fish Creek Mountain.

"I can tell you I've never been here," Cal said, breaking the silence.

"No, few hikers are out here," Lil said as she took a drink of water. "We still have a way to go."

The two continued for another hour in silence.

"Cal, I know you told me a little about your grandmother. What can you tell me about her?" Lil said.

Cal wasn't sure why Lil brought up his grandmother, but happy to break the silence. "Not too much to tell. She died before I was born. My grandfather would talk about her a lot. I know she loved these mountains. When my grandfather would take me on hikes, he seemed to speak of her nonstop."

"You said she was Native American?" Lil asked.

"Yes. My grandfather said her parents weren't happy that she married him, but they eventually accepted him, at least until she died."

"You said your father would point out some writings you came across," Lil asked.

"Right. Like the one, we've come across many times. The hunters and the longhorn sheep and a larger white hunter above them."

"A white warrior, not a hunter," Lil paused, "as the story is told."

The two came up to a narrow ledge as they were getting higher up the mountain.

"Here we are, Cal," Lil said as they approached a large crack between large boulders.

17

In January 1961, a body was found by a group of children who were picnicking in the Superstition Mountains. The man had a bullet hole in his back and it was thought the body was there for approximately a year. The body was later identified as Hilmer Bohen, a prospector from Salt Lake City.[1]

* * *

Jose had made his way to the Cliff Dwelling in Rogers Canyon. The directions Cal gave him on the location and room were spot on. Jose got to the far wall where he saw the large stone that, unless one was looking for it, would blend in.

He slid the stone over and sure enough, as Cal had told him, there would be a small tunnel. Jose hoisted himself up and turned on his flashlight, and proceeded down the tunnel. Jose wasn't in the tunnel for over ten minutes until he came to a clay brick wall. In the light, it wasn't easy to determine the age of the bricks but as Jose pushed on the wall, he could tell they weren't as brittle as the adobe fixture he came from.

Jose pushed the wall in a few places and even tried to remove some bricks. Within a few minutes, one brick broke and Jose flashed the light in the hole. It was another layer of bricks. Jose pushed harder on the wall and it didn't move a bit. Who knew how many layers the wall was?

Jose turned back and headed back to the cliff dwelling and placed the large stone back in place. He wanted to let Cal know what he found. Jose pulled out his cell phone and as he expected, no service. He sent a text as it would automatically send once he regained service.

"Cal, I'm at the cliff dwelling. It appears someone has been very busy, as the tunnel has been sealed up. Call me when you get a chance."

* * *

"Cal, please be open-minded and take my lead. Eventually, you will understand." Lil said to Cal as she then took a step around a blind bend in the canyon.

Cal followed her and he thought he heard voices in the distance. He also thought he smelled some smoke. As he followed Lil around the bend, he saw numerous structures built into the narrow canyon walls, and below was a small stream.

Sure enough, just like the kids had told him about the people in the cave, here as well it appeared to be a community of indigenous people.

"So the kids were right?" Cal said.

"Yes. They weren't supposed to stumble on the village by the Rodgers Canyon." Lil said.

"But they did. They won't be the last." Cal paused. "I have to wonder who else came across them and what happened to them. Were they the ones trying to break into Freddy's room?"

"The kids were in no danger. They just wanted to talk to them and erase their photos," Lil said. She thought about months back, taking the SD card from Jennifer and erasing photos she had taken of one of these people.

"They have no right to break and enter," Cal snapped back.

"They didn't break in. They were at Freddy's window trying to get his attention." Lil said.

"Are you going to tell me these people living here don't have anything to do with some of the crazy shit that happens in these mountains?" Cal said as he looked out over the structures.

"I will not say who did what to whom over the last few hundred years here. The Native American tribes fought each other, the Spaniards came through looking for gold, followed then by Mexicans and the white man. They all wanted something from these mountains."

"How long do you, do they, think they can continue to live here? This is a National Forest." Cal said.

"It's getting more difficult over the last twenty-five years. More hikers, more aircraft, drones, a lot going on," Lil said as she took a step and reached out to take Cal's hand. "It's time for you to meet some people."

The two walked down to the base of one of the structures on one side of the cliff.

"This is the Great House, the main village," Lil explained.

Cal watched as several young men brought containers of water to a variety of locations throughout this village. Cal just stopped and couldn't believe what he was seeing. How could this be unseen for so long?

They continued to walk to where a few women were cooking. A few older women were sitting near the fire and appeared to be making blankets.

"Cal, I want you to meet some people," Lil continued as they turned into a small room, "They are expecting us."

In the room were three men and two women all much older than both Cal and Lil.

"Welcome, Cal," said the oldest man sitting in the middle.

"We knew this day was coming, but we thought it wouldn't be for a while," the woman to the far right said.

"We understand you were thrown into this situation hastily. I know Liluye has shared with you a lot about the Superstition Mountains, the Thunder Mountains as we call them. But she didn't have the time to share with you everything," said the other woman.

"Share the hidden secrets," said one of the remaining men.

"We are the hidden secret," the eldest man in the middle continued. "The hidden secret of the Superstitions. Although the white man believes the Salado culture disappeared, this is proof," he said, raising his hands, "That we are alive and far from extinct."

Cal looked around the room and smiled at the group. "It's a pleasure to meet you all. This is a bit of a shock, I guess I would say."

"Our people have been here for 3000 years. Many have tried to remove us. We have fought, died, and killed to keep our land. As many died to keep it, even more, were taken away, but we are all that remains. Just under five hundred of us scattered in these mountains," the old man stated.

"My grandfather took me up to these mountains frequently. He would share stories with me. Sometimes his friends would join us or meet us and they would share some. My grandmother was Native American, so I understand the flight of your people. I guess my people. My grandfather and parents made sure I understood my roots. I never met my grandmother, but I wish I had," Cal said to the group.

"We are in desperate times. We need your help," the woman on the far right said.

"This is a National Forest. I'm not sure you'll be allowed to stay here. Frankly, I'm not sure what I can do. Lil is probably in a better place to help you than I am," Cal said emphatically to the group.

"Liluye has been a great help. She has done her job splendidly and she still has work to do, but it is time for a new direction."

"Have you reached out to any authorities? Letting someone help you?" Cal asked.

"They, like you, would probably think that every dead body found in the Superstitions was the result of our doing. Deputy Ligai, I can assure you we knew this day was coming and we have not killed anyone in quite some time. We need to find a peaceful solution," the man to the left explained.

"I wouldn't say I thought you were killing people, but there are a lot of killings and beheadings in these mountains," Cal answered.

"Yes, there have been. Most deaths are the white men killing each other or just accidents." One of the women answered.

"It is written that the White Warrior will help us in our time of need. He will come to us. The stars are aligned," the older man said, pointing to the painting on the ceiling. "That time is now. Deputy Ligai, you are the White Warrior."

Cal shook his head. "I'm sorry you've got the wrong person. I'll help if I can. I can reach out to people, but I can't make any promises and I can assure you I'm not any White Warrior."

The five elders looked at each other as the woman to the far right spoke. "Deputy Ligai, it's a lot to take in. Please think about it and if you go to anyone, keep in mind the consequences our people, your people, will have. Liluye will be an excellent resource and of course, we will talk with you anytime you would like."

The elders continued to tell Cal the history of the people in the Superstitions. Eventually, Lil turned to Cal and stood up.

"I will honor your request and give this some great thought, but you must also realize I am an officer to the county and country I live in. I have a lot to think about and weigh the options that are best for all." Cal said as he approached all the members and shook hands.

As Cal followed Lil to the door and then turned to the group as the old man looked into Cal's eyes. "There is no denying what is written. You are the White Warrior."

An older woman stopped Cal and Lil as they were making their way out of the village, back to the entrance they came in.

"I heard you were coming," she said as she looked up into Cal's eyes. "I'm glad I caught you before you left. You probably have a lot of thoughts running through your head," as she grabbed Cal's hand.

Cal looked into the old woman's eyes. "Yes. It is a lot to absorb. I'm not sure I can do much to help. Hopefully, I can reach out to some people who can help you."

"Don't let them take us off our land. Weigh out all your decisions, then be decisive. Be like the eagle, visionary, determined, and," the old woman said as Cal finished her sentence.

"Deliberate. My grandfather would say that to me about eagles."

"Yes, deliberate," she said, releasing his hand.

"We must go," Cal said as he turned to Lil and they left the village that was tucked in the cliffs of the canyon.

Lil and Cal walked for a good thirty minutes without saying anything. Cal was trying to figure out what to do as he was being pulled in a variety of directions. He turned a few times as he thought they were being followed but saw no one.

They finally stopped to drink some water. Cal took a seat on a small boulder facing Lil. He couldn't believe how, in an instant, his world was turned upside down.

He looked up at Lil, who was standing in front of him, "So you've been in on this the entire time? You've been playing me?"

"Yes and no," Lil continued. "These are my people, so I've been involved my entire life. No, I have not been playing you. Guiding you, making sure you saw what you needed to see."

"I'm not sure what I needed to know and see. I definitely wanted to find out about the missing hikers. The rest is overwhelming." Cal paused, looking into the mountains, the mountains that contained so many mysteries.

Cal looked into Lil's eyes, "And probably the least important part, but damn it hurts, you and I. I fell in love with you."

"It's not the least important. As you will learn, it will be the most important. I am in love with you as well. Yes, it was my job to guide you so you see your destiny," Lil said as her eyes teared up.

"My destiny? What is everyone talking about?" Cal raised his voice as he stood up.

"Do you remember on our first hike we came across a drawing? A drawing that had a large white warrior overlooking all the other people?" Lil asked.

"Yes," Cal replied.

"And you've seen that drawing many times, correct?"

"Well, once you pointed it out, it seems I saw it weekly," Cal replied.

"And as a child, when you were with your grandfather, did you see it then?" Lil continued.

Cal thought back about his hikes and it came to him in an instant. He had seen it numerous times. His grandfather had pointed it out to him many times as well.

"What the hell is this about, yes I saw it as a child," Cal said.

"I told you it has been foreseen that the great white warrior of life will protect our people, our mountain. The legend speaks of a time when they are discovered after hiding for hundreds of years. The white warrior will protect us all." Lil said as she stepped closer to Cal. "Cal, you are the white warrior of life."

"You're frigging crazy. This is crazy," Cal said, wanting to grab Lil and shake her and wake up out of a dream.

"Cal, you know your grandmother was Native American. Her lineage was to produce this warrior to help our people. Your grandfather understood what was at stake. He wanted to take the first step in getting you ready. My responsibility was to take it further and make sure you can run with this," Lil said as she took a step closer and placed her hand on Cal's chest.

"So let me get this, because I'm part Native American, predominately Caucasian. I'm the white warrior," Cal asked.

"No, although your bloodline plays a major role, not because you're considered a white man. Do you know what your name means?" Lil asked, looking into his eyes.

"Ligai? It's Russian, that's all I know." Cal said, grasping Lil's hand.

"Yes but translated into the tongue of Native Americans from this area, it means white," Lil said.

"Come on, so my name means white. You need to do better than that." Cal retorted.

"And your first name?" Lil asked.

"Cal, what are you going to tell me about the name Cal?" he replied.

"Not Cal, but Calian," Lil said as he looked at Lil bewildered and stepped back as Lil continued. "Cal, what is the name on your birth certificate?"

"How did you know that? It is Calian." Cal replied in disbelief.

"In our native tongue, Calian means Warrior of Life. Calian Ligai means the White Warrior of Life. Cal, you are here to protect our people. Protect our way of life, protect our sacred land."

"Anything else you want to share with me?" Cal asked Lil.

"No. I think there was a lot to digest there. I'm sorry." Lil replied.

"Lil, I can't act like I don't know about all these people here. You can't expect me to keep a secret that there is a tribe living in the Superstition Mountains. That there are individuals, such as you, that work for federal and state agencies helping keep this hidden. Let alone the crimes involved in doing this," Cal said as he regained his composure.

"Cal, first there have been no crimes," Lil replied.

"Kidnapping, for one," Cal snapped back.

"And who was kidnapped? Lil said.

"Bob Kravis, Michael Kowalski, Linda Sharper. You tell me," Cal snapped back.

"You are making some very large assumptions, Cal," Lil answered.

"You know this is not right. I just can't sit on this. You understand that," Cal said, looking into Lil's eyes. "I have to turn you in."

"You will do what you feel is right. I just ask you to think it over," Lil said as she reached out and held his arm.

"Lil, you know I've fallen in love with you. I'll give you twenty-four hours before I report this."

"Cal, do what you must, but there is more to the story. It is written you are the White Warrior of Life. You are not alone in this. It is written that I will be your wife and we will have a daughter, the guardian of the Superstitions."

Cal walked back to the trail which led to his car. He felt drunk. He felt like he was just in a fight that he lost. His mind was spinning, and he did not know what to do next. There was a part of him that knew what he needed to do. The other part was to wait, at least till his head was clear.

Lil let Cal go on his own. She knew he needed to make this decision by himself. He knew what he saw. He knew some of the history and she hoped he knew how she felt about him. She wasn't worried about what would happen to her. She wasn't worried about if Cal brought this out into the open and what secrets he was going to share, she was just worried about how he was taking all this thrown at him.

Later that evening, Cal found himself sitting at the bar of a small pub in Apache Junction. The first drink was to relax him. The next few were to help him decide what was the right thing to do.

He had fallen for Lil and it turns out he was just being used. She said she had feelings for him, but he couldn't make himself believe that. She worked for the National Forest. He was a County Deputy. He had a responsibility to let his supervisor know what was going on,

Then he still didn't know how the missing hikers played into this, if at all. Was it something random? But if so, why were people calling their families pretending to be the authorities?

Then add into the equation that these people thought he was part of some prophecy to help them stay hidden. Lil was caught up in the entire thing and there still had to be something else. It still didn't make any sense.

As the thoughts bounced in his head, he wished there was someone to talk to. Jose seemed like the logical choice, but once he would be brought into this situation, there would be no turning back.

Cal took a sip of his whiskey. "You look like you had a hard day," came a voice next to him.

Cal turned to a couple that was sitting by his side. "Yeah. It's been a tough one." Cal said as he shifted his body to them.

"Life is filled with them. Usually after a good night's sleep, things look better," the woman said, who sat beyond her partner.

"I'm not sure sleep will help unless I wake up and everything was a dream," Cal replied.

"We've both been there. Sometimes it's life-altering. But if you sit back and look at it, if you make your decision on what is best for all parties. Be determined and deliberate," the woman said.

Cal looked at her, puzzled. "Those are words I heard earlier today, words I've heard before," Cal responded, still bewildered to hear her say those same words he heard a few hours ago.

"They are good words," the man said.

"Yes, they are," Cal continued. "Well, I'm off home where I can't do too much damage. Pleasure speaking with you. Cal Ligai," Cal said as he placed his hand out.

"Mike," the man returned the shake as the woman put out her hand.

"Lynda. Cal, a good night's rest, and I bet you see things more clearly," the woman said with a warm smile.

Cal smiled back, laid his money on the bar, and left the pub. He wasn't sure he had any idea what he should do, but if the woman was right, it was waiting till the morning. Things could look different.

18

In March 1961, a body filled with bullet holes was found in Needle Canyon. He was later identified as Walter Mowry from Denver Colorado.[1]

* * *

Cal had one more drink when he got home and eventually fell asleep on the couch. His dreams were filled with the previous day's encounters. In his dream, the five elders he met all had a mask on. They addressed Cal as the White Warrior. In the dream, he knew he was the White Warrior and was going to help his people.

The older woman he had met outside kept coming into the building, whispering into Cal's ear. He would turn to her and then she was gone, but only to return several more times. She had whispered to Cal to go into the next room and find the answers. Cal nodded to the five masked figures and entered the next room.

There the room had transformed into a bar, one very similar to the one he was in last night. There at the bar were sat, Lynda and Mike. Cal approached them and the three smiled.

"Lynda, Mike, I'm glad to see you again," Cal said in his dream.

Cal woke suddenly. Lynda, Mike, or was it Linda and Michael? Linda Sharper and Michael Kowalski? It couldn't be. Just his mind playing tricks on him and his dream. Cal sat up and tried to shake the dream, but he couldn't. He finally got up and splashed water on his face. Cal looked out at the moonlit sky and then made his way to his desk in the far bedroom. He pulled the files on Linda Sharper and Michael Kowalski and did some math. Could it be them? Were they the correct ages? He wasn't sure, but he thought it was a possibility.

He looked at the clock. It was only a few minutes past 2 AM and he felt like he didn't get any sleep. He made his way to his bed and, as his head hit the pillow, he fell asleep. Cal had more peaceful dreams the remainder of the night, and by the time he would be awake for a few minutes, they would escape his memory.

* * *

Lil had spent all evening and into the early hours of the morning stopping at the villages within the Superstitions. She wanted to make sure contingent plans were understood if Cal was to go to the authorities. She was surviving strictly on adrenaline, driving to multiple locations, all of which had several-mile hikes from the road.

She didn't know what Cal was going to do. If they only had more time to transition Cal into what he found out today. It was too much for one person to take, and there was still more. Somehow the future of the Native American Tribe that called the Superstition Mountains their home fell on Calian Ligai, the White Warrior.

It was 3 am when she was headed back to her pickup from the last village and two men walked with her on the dark hike. They used limited light so as not to be seen, but they all knew there were certain spots that even the brightest moon lite wouldn't be enough.

They whispered details to each other as they all knew how the voices carry in the wind at night. As they approached Lil's vehicle, the one changed the subject.

"Liluye, will Cal save us or turn us in?"

"It is written he will protect us, but I don't know if that time is now or in the future. We will wait and see. We have done all we can. If the government gets involved, we will move quietly in the night." Lil replied.

She got into her pickup and pulled away, too tired to realize that someone was watching her, someone was listening.

* * *

The figure hidden by the trailhead sat quietly for hours. Waiting to find out what was going on. Maybe it would be better if he had some backup, but there was no proof. He scanned the mountains to the east as he felt confident that the people he saw would be coming from.

But even if people came out, what would that prove? They take hikes in the dark. The hidden figure then saw a flicker of light heading toward him. He could hear voices, but couldn't make anything out. He finally saw three figures move towards a pickup and their conversation could be heard more clearly.

"We have done all we can. If the government gets involved, we will move quietly in the night," came the female voice. The hidden figure knew it was the voice of Ranger Shanta.

* * *

Cal's eyes opened to the bright sun flooding his room. Cal was wondering how late it was as he glanced at the clock. 6:12 am but in Arizona, the Sun is always up early.

He didn't get the amount of sleep he was hoping for, but he felt better. His mind was racing, his body was pounding from within. He went into the kitchen to make some coffee. Time to regroup his thoughts.

He needed to departmentalize everything, a group of people living in the Superstition Mountains. Did they commit any crimes, that they feel he is their White Warrior, and what this all means about him and Lil?

The first cup of water had made it through the coffee filter and Cal wasn't waiting any longer as he poured his first cup. These people, although have been there for hundreds of years, would be relocated just as so many Native Americans were in the past. Unless legislation could put an injunction on them being moved. That would take a lot of time and could be too little too late.

Besides trespassing, what crimes did they commit? Is there any association with all the death and missing people in the Superstitions? Hard to tell and even more difficult to prove. That one he would have to go back to. Then the dream. His dream where he was speaking to Mike and Lynda. Were they Michael Kowalski and Linda Sharper? That's the first question for Lil.

This entire thing about being the White Warrior was next on his mind, and he gulped down the last of his first mug of coffee. As Cal got up to refill his cup, he couldn't help but chuckle. Him a White Warrior, a leader for these people who he only met yesterday. That was an easy one to answer. He was not who they thought he is but as he sat down, he was thinking he was going to help them, help them stay in their homes.

Finally, what did this all mean about him and Lil? He felt so betrayed and blindsided. He had finally let down his walls and this. She said she loved him, but there was a lot to examine in their relationship. Although emotionally he wanted to solve this quickly, he knew this could wait till everything else was taken care of.

A quick shower and then head to work. He still wasn't sure about bringing anyone into this until he at least could speak to Lil and get some answers. After that, who to bring in on this? Going to the sheriff or Sergeant Melkin would only force them to take immediate action. Maybe he could hold off a few days to get some things in motion to keep the people of the Superstitions from being taken away.

He grabbed his phone and sent a text to Lil, "Can we talk tonight?" and then he headed to the shower.

Cal sat at his desk, reading Jose's text that the tunnel was filled in. He knew why, but how was he going to explain this to Jose? He wasn't ready to yet. Cal pulled the files of Linda Sharper and Michael Kowalski. Both files had a photo of them years ago and although it could be them, it was just too difficult to determine from last night.

He was glad it was quiet, with nothing of urgency. Cal would head to the Superstitions and make sure there weren't any hikers not prepared for the mountain. He glanced at his phone, but still no reply from Lil.

Cal knew he had to address Jose's text and let him know where he was if something were to come up. A phone call would be best. Cal got in his truck and dialed Jose.

"Brother!" Jose answered Cal could feel his smile over the phone.

"Hey, man, I'm sorry about not getting back to you till now. Something came up."

"No worries, man. I knew if you didn't get back to me, there was a good reason. I'm not sure I was any help. The tunnel I found was all sealed up." Jose said.

"I'm sorry for wasting your time. I must have mixed up the locations. There was a blocked tunnel as well. Anyway, I got into the office early and am now headed out. Everything seems quiet. I figured I'd go to the Superstitions and see if anybody had seen Jeff Albright in the mountains over the last few weeks." Cal said.

"Aren't you the early bird? Sounds like a plan. I'll stick around the office in case something pops up." Jose answered.

"Okay, thanks. I'll check in later."

Cal disconnected the call and saw there was a text message on his phone.

"Do you have a few minutes to talk this morning?" the text read.

It was not from Lil but from Waylen.

* * *

Cal pulled into the diner parking lot and headed in. He saw Waylen sitting in a booth towards the back and headed over.

"Cal, thanks for taking a few minutes," Waylen said as he reached across the table to shake Cal's hand.

"No worries. What can I do for you?" Cal asked, wondering what this was all about.

"First, let me say you're not going to like what I have to say. Second, I could have gone to multiple people on this, but I came to you," Waylen continued. "I really have very little proof to go on and I hope you can prove me wrong."

Cal tried to show Waylen his best poker face. Had Waylen figured out about the people in the Superstitions?

"Somehow I figured I wouldn't like it. Let's have it." Cal snickered.

"I was hiking in the Superstitions last night. I saw some flickering lights. But it wasn't someone walking or an open fire. It was a code. I have no idea what it meant, but I tried to find where it was coming from. I narrowed it down to a trailhead and figured I would wait. Not sure for what, but I had a funny feeling."

Cal's thoughts went immediately to the coded lights he had seen numerous times from Lil's home. "So, what did you find? More coded flickers?"

"I saw some lights headed towards me, but it wasn't any kind of code, just for vision. I think I came across a smuggling operation," Waylen said.

"What kind of smuggling, drugs, people? And, yes, why come to me and not the sheriff?"

"I don't know what they are smuggling, but I heard one of them say, "We have done all we can. If the government gets involved, move quietly in the night, Or something like that. Why I came to you is I recognized the voice. I was Lil Shanta."

Cal continued to appear as emotionless as possible. "Are you sure it was Lil Shanta? Could you see her?" he asked.

"I couldn't see her, but I know that voice and it was the same type of pickup," Waylen continued. "Look, I know you think the world of her. For me, there is something not right, but I don't want any of us to be involved in some smuggling. So if anyone can find out and clear her, I figure it would be you. If you can't and she's guilty, she'll deserve whatever she gets."

"I appreciate you coming to me. There is no way she is doing any type of smuggling. I'll find out what's going on. Give me some time." Cal replied.

"Well, that's it. I can't wait too long, maybe a few days, then I'm placing myself in way too much jeopardy."

"That's fair. Just don't reach out to anyone till you talk to me," Cal said as he ran his fingers through his hair.

"Yep, a few days. Honestly, I hope she is innocent." Waylen said as he rose from the table, then exited.

Cal pulled out his phone. Still no reply from Lil. He sent her another message. "You were spotted last night. Urgent we talk." He hit send and then paced a ten-dollar bill on the table and left himself.

Waylen added one more thing to worry about. Cal needed to move quickly. He headed to Dutchman State Park, as he knew most Tuesdays Lil was there. As he drove down Route 88, Cal was having flashbacks of times when his grandfather took him into the Superstitions. He would share with him stories and now it came back to Cal, the story of the White Warrior.

At the time, it made little sense and frankly, it still sounded crazy to Cal, but it was all like a nightmare he couldn't wake up from. He pulled into the park and went to one of the main parking lots. In the far corner, he saw a Tonto Forest pickup. He pulled up to the truck and then headed up to the trails.

He pulled out his binoculars and finally, he saw an image of a Park Ranger near Treasure Loop trail. As he made his way closer, it appeared to be Ranger McTavish.

"Shawn, how are things?" Cal asked as he approached McTavish.

"Pretty good. A quiet morning." He replied.

"Hey, do you know where Lil is?"

"She is normally here today, but she called in. Can I help you with anything?'

"Okay, I thought this was her day to be at the park. No worries, nothing of urgency," Cal said, and he made his way back to his truck.

* * *

With Cal in the field and things quiet, Jose used the time to review his reports and tidy up a few loose ends. He came across the file on Jeff Albright. The autopsy confirmed he died from a blow to the head. Marks on the body showed the body was moved, but that was all they could tell. The body had no other evidence and the severe elements of the Superstitions, even for a short period, washed away the scene of evidence.

It looked like another homicide in the Superstition Mountains. The sheriff's department officially took over the case. The SAR continued to monitor anything suspicious. Local fliers and social media posting on information came up with only a few leads that led nowhere.

The Superstitions took enough human life, which was even worse when it was someone being murdered. Since Cal had joined the team, Cal had shared some of the crazy unsolved mysteries that Jose rarely paid attention to, but maybe there was something to it.

As if the sheriff was reading Jose's mind, the sheriff called Jose into his office.

"Jose, I was wondering if we can borrow your expertise on the Superstitions and we put you on the team to investigate the body we found a few days ago. If there is a major search and rescue operation that will take priority over this. I'm not sure what we'll find. Frankly, I'd love to find out some animal dragged the body versus a killer in the mountains," the sheriff said.

"You got it, sir. I agree with you on that. I'll keep you posted." Jose replied.

*   *   *

Cal's phone vibrated as he picked it up and saw it was a text from Lil. "I'm off today. I can meet any time."

"Can we meet at your house when I get off? I can be there by six," Cal replied to Lil.

Cal looked at the time on his phone. He still had another four hours before he could start asking Lil some questions he came up with this morning. And now he had to add to it what Waylen heard. He was hoping it remained quiet the rest of the afternoon, no injured hiker, no lost person in one of the canyons.

Cal' stopped at several trailheads showing photos of Jeff Albright and if anyone had seen him a few weeks back. His mind was split between finding answers on this hiker and the people living in the mountains he was exposed to yesterday.

Cal's phone rang and he saw it was an incoming call from Jose. "What's up," Cal answered.

"Brother, any luck with the fliers?" Jose asked.

"No. Pretty quiet out here today."

"Okay. I also wanted to let you know the sheriff is having me split a good amount of my time to help get some answers to Albright. So the entire team's rotation might change for a bit."

"Really. Any leads?" Cal asked.

"Not one. I think that's why they want my help." Jose answered.

"Well, anything I can help with, let me know."

"You got it. Talk to you later." Jose said before ending the call.

One more thing to add to the equation, Cal thought. For every step forward there seems to be one or two back. His mind felt clearer but there were still too many unanswered questions and it seemed he was being pulled in numerous directions.

Cal headed back to Florence, checked his mail, jumped into his car, and headed to Lil. The drive appeared longer than normal. The sunset on the Superstitions gave the rocks that pink, mysterious feel.

Lil was waiting at the front door when he arrived. As she opened the door, she extended her arm towards the living room.

"Cal, have a seat. I'm sure you have a lot of questions." She said, sitting on the couch as Cal sat on the large chair.

Cal sat on the edge of the chair. "Yes, I have a few. I'm only interested in the truth."

"I understand. That's all you'll get from me," Lil said as she placed her hands on her knees.

"No specific order, I guess. There have been a lot of people killed in the Superstitions and maybe even more people have gone missing. What and how are the people I met yesterday responsible for?" Cal asked.

"We all know it's a deadly mountain range. The Native Americans have killed each other for hundreds of years. When the Spaniards came, the Native American people did whatever they had to get rid of the intruders. When the Mexicans came, they killed some just as they had when the white man first appeared. But I can assure you they have killed no one in the last fifty to sixty years."

"What about this Jeff Albright? Did they kill him.?"

"No. They moved his body. They found him dead very close to an entrance to one of the villages. But he was dead when they found him." Lil answered.

"Okay, what about all the missing people? Surely they have a hand in some of that." Cal said as he sat back in the chair.

"They have. But not what you think. There have been some people who have stumbled across our villages. They are asked for their silence or to join us. We have had some people decide to live the more wholesome experience, one with nature, and have joined us."

"Bob Kravis," Cal raised his eyes.

"Yes, he lives in the Superstition."

"Michael Kowalski, Linda Sharper.?"

"Yes, they live in the Superstitions as well," Lil said calmly.

"Did I meet them last night?" Cal said as he sat on the edge of the chair again.

"From what I was told, it was a good talk,"

Cal stood up. "Jesus Christ, everyone is playing me for a fool!"

"Not at all. Everyone thought you should see for yourself that your imagination may be worse than reality."

Cal paced the living room floor. "Anything else on that matter before I move on to their legal rights to be there?" Cal said as he then stood still, looking at Lil.

"Just one more thing. The older woman you met yesterday. She's your grandmother."

Cal slowly sat back in the chair in total disbelief. "So everyone has lied to me. You, two strangers in a bar, now my grandmother. She threw away her life she could have had with me to be in the mountains." Cal said as he got choked up.

"Everyone needed to make sacrifices. She played an important job in keeping the people safe and at the same time preparing you as the White Warrior."

"Okay, we can stop with the White Warrior shit. That's not me. You're all nuts." Cal said as his eyes became moist.

"Eventually you will see. It has been written." Lil said as she reached over and placed her hand on his.

Cal looked up at Lil. "We have another problem. Waylen overheard you last night at a trailhead talking about evading the US Government. He thinks you're involved in some smuggling operation. I have to clear your name pretty damn fast or he's going to others."

"What the hell was that bastard doing following me?" Lil said in disgust.

"Dumb luck. I think he came across the lights you must use to communicate. Like the ones I've seen many times from here." Cal replied.

"Shit. He has been nothing but a pain in the ass. You have to tell him he heard it wrong, you have to convince him. Or it wasn't me, it was someone else."

"And one more thing," Cal said as he felt it was Lil's turn to get all the bad news. "Jose has been assigned to find out about Jeff Albright and look for any clues or anomalies in the mountains. If Waylen gets a hold of him, this is going to turn into a cluster fast."

"Cal, do you have any questions about us?" Lil asked as she gained her composure.

"Right now I feel played. Maybe your feelings are genuine, maybe not, but right now we have to keep Jose,

Waylen, or anyone from finding out about the villages until we can come up with a solution, a legal one."

"So you will help us?" Lil said with a smile.

"Yes," Cal smiled back

"It is written," Lil said with a smirk.

19

In the Fall of 1961, a search was organized for Jabez Clapp, a hermit prospector, who had been missing in the Superstition mountains. After an extensive search, it was called off and it wasn't until three years later that the headless remains of Jabez Clapp were found near Weavers Needle.[1]

* * *

The next morning, Cal woke with clear objectives for the day. Reach out to the kids and make sure they were okay. And remind them not to say anything to anyone, at least till he had some time to figure things out.

The next thing was to speak with Waylen. He still wasn't sure what he was going to say, but he needed to defuse the situation. The next was to find out what Jose was thinking and try to keep him from running across any of the villages. And from there he had to find someone at a high level he could trust to see if there was a legal action to take. He did not know who that person would be. On top of all that, he was working.

By mid-morning, two hikers had serious falls up Siphon Draw on the way to Flatiron. The first was close to the top and they had broken their leg. Cal and one of the volunteers were able to assist the hiker to the top, where a helicopter picked them up and transported them to a local hospital.

The second hiker was on their way up as Cal was working his way down. The hiker had numerous scrapes and mild contusions, but after a few minutes, seemed able to turn back down to the parking lot. Cal walked with the hiker and their party until they were in their vehicle.

Cal sent a text to Sarah, "I'm just checking in on you and your brother. I'm still fact-checking a few things. Are you guys fine?"

Sarah returned the message immediately. "We're good… Still a bit in shock at what we came across…."

"Did you speak to your parents about this yet?" Cal replied.

"No, not yet," Sarah replied.

"I think I should tell them, or at least be with you…"

"They'll freak out."

"We need to tell them. If I'm there, I can answer any concerns they'll have. Will everyone be home this evening?"

"Yes…"

"Sarah, tell your parent I'll be stopping over at six with an update…" Cal replied.

Cal then sent a text to Waylen, "I'm at Dutchman State Park, helping a few hikers. I think I heard you were at Peralta?..." Cal texted.

A few minutes later, Waylen replied, "Situation under control... leaving the trailhead now..."

"If you have a few minutes, I have an update..." Cal.

"Yes. I'll be passing by the coffee shop near the library... meet in the parking lot?" Waylen.

"See you there..."

Within fifteen minutes, Cal was parked in the lot of the "Coffee Quench". It was only a few minutes before Cal saw Waylen's pickup pull into the parking lot as he pulled up next to him. The two men got out of their vehicles and met behind them.

"Waylen, thanks for meeting me. I spoke with Lil. You're right, it was her up there. I told her you saw her last night," Cal said, still not sure how this was going to all play out.

"And what did she say?" Waylen asked as his eyes squinted in the sun.

"She really wishes she knew you were there,"

"I bet," Waylen snickered.

"She said she could have used your help."

"I doubt that," Waylen snapped back.

"Lil had seen some flickering lights as well and went to check it out. She came across a couple of shady guys. They said they were camping overnight. They insisted on walking her back to her vehicle."

"What about her comment on the government and moving quietly in the night?" Waylen inquired.

"She was trying to scare them and telling them about government law enforcement scanning the mountains, even at nighttime. She said she was concerned for her safety." Cal went on. He could see that Waylen seemed to have bought it.

"Did she report it to anyone?' Waylen asked.

"I would guess. I didn't ask," Cal answered.

"I'm sorry. I should have come forward. Anything I should do?"

"I think it's all taken care of. The Forest Rangers will monitor anything going on. I've got to make a call Waylen now, sorry. Thanks for meeting me. I'm sure we'll see each other soon enough in the mountains," Cal said, forcing a smile.

Cal had a few more hours before he met with Sarah and Freddy's parents. The Apache Junction Police Department was right around the corner. Cal wanted to defuse any spotlight on the boy from the Superstitions outside of Freddy's room.

No time like the present, Cal thought as he headed to the AJ Police station. He entered the station and made his way to the front desk and introduced himself.

"I've got some insight on the call the other night on Desert Ave. They called on trespassing. The Campbell family." Cal said.

The sergeant at the front desk typed in a few things. "Here it is. You're in luck. One of the officers, Deputy Roberts, is here. Would you like to speak with him?"

"That would be great, thanks," Cal said as he stepped back and waited for Deputy Roberts to come out.

A few minutes later, a large burly man approached Cal. "Deputy Ligai, I understand you have some information on the Campbell call the other night?"

"Yes. I know the family a bit. Well, the kids hike in the mountains and we were looking for the boy, Freddy, a few months ago. Anyway, it turns out the person who was trespassing was a boy that Freddy Campbell had met. He got a bit startled when the lights came on and Freddy's sister screamed."

"Okay. Are Campbell's aware of this," the officer inquired.

"I'm meeting the family this evening. I have to speak to the parents about the kids' hike. I'll let them know it was his friend Naiche."

Deputy Rogers pulled out a pad and started scribbling down some notes. "Naiche? What kind of name is that? What's his last name? Do you have an address?"

"I'm not sure of the last name. I want to say, Johnstone. I don't have an address. The kid is hiking all the time in the Superstitions. Friendly kid, a bit different though," Cal said.

"If you could find out that information, it would be great. I'll make a note that we spoke," Deputy Rogers said as he placed out his hand to shake Cal's.

Cal's head was still spinning. So much had happened in the last few days. He still felt pulled in numerous directions and even when he felt he was making a sound decision, part of him thought he wasn't doing the right thing, mainly to the Sheriff's department. He knew he was on the clock. At some point soon, he needed to get the authorities involved.

Cal dropped off his truck at the Sheriff's office. Jose had taken off for the day. Cal knew Jose would be busy looking into what happened to Jeff Albright, but he wanted to share much of what happened with him. The time wasn't right, and maybe this was all happening for a reason.

Within the hour, Cal pulled in front of the Campbell's residence. He introduced himself to Sarah and Freddy's parents, and they invited him into their living room.

"I'm happy to say that we have found out who was in your yard the other night. Freddy and Sarah have become quite the hikers in the mountains."

"I hope they aren't getting into any trouble up there," their mother inquired.

"No. I wish more children were outdoors to enjoy this beautiful land we live in. On their hikes, Freddy has met with another young man who is in the mountains. It was this young man who was in your yard. He was trying to wake up Freddy. He became a bit startled when Sarah saw him." Cal said.

"Why are you telling us," the father continued, "You're with Search and Rescue."

"I know the young man, Naiche. He's aware that he caused some concern. I can assure you it won't happen again. I was speaking with Deputy Rogers of the Apache Junction Police Department and spoke to him about this as well."

The mother turned to her children and then her husband, "Maybe you shouldn't be hiking in the mountains, it's so dangerous."

"The Superstition Mountains are a place to respect and be aware of your surroundings. From what I have seen, your children are mindful of where they are. The other reason I'm here is that your children came across a small adobe village in the mountains. The Tonto Forest is looking into this site. It's really an impressive find." Cal said as he made eye contact with the entire family.

"Were there people? Was Naiche's family there?" Freddy asked.

"No. It appears to be abandoned now. There will be a more thorough look at the site. We are hoping few people learn about this site before we can find more information." Cal continued as he stood up.

"Anyway, your kids found an interesting place in the mountains. Very exciting and as I said, Naiche, who Freddy and Sarah had met on the trails, was the boy in your yard."

"I wish he would have texted or called like most kids these days," their mother said.

Sarah remained quiet as she understood what Officer Ligai was sharing and more important what he was not saying. She felt better knowing who was in their yard. and that her parents were aware of what Freddy had come across, even if they didn't know everything.

Cal left the Campbell's home and headed to Lil's. He hadn't sent her a text that he would stop by, but he felt she would expect him. Sure enough, as he proceeded up her walkway, she opened the door to let him in.

"I was hoping you would be coming over," Lil said as she cautiously smiled at Cal.

"I have a lot to figure out and not much time. I don't like keeping secrets. I'm jeopardizing my career with all of this," Cal replied.

"Let me get you a drink," Lil said as she poured two small glasses of bourbon.

"I spoke with Waylen. I told him you saw blinking lights as well and you went to check them out. You found people who were camping overnight and they walked you back to your pickup," Cal said as he took the drink from Lil.

"Did he buy it? What about what he heard.?"

"I told him you had a feeling they might be a bit shady, so you were trying to let them know the mountains were under surveillance by different agencies. He seemed to believe me."

"Let's hope so. I also spoke to the Campbell family and the Apache Police Department. I told them I knew the boy in their yard and, for the most part, harmless and he was just trying to get Freddy's attention." Cal continued. "I'm supposed to get the boy's full name and address. Maybe you can help me with that?"

"We have a few addresses. We should be able to figure something out," Lil said as she took a sip of her drink. "Are you going to the authorities about what you've seen?"

"I feel I have to. They shouldn't be living there, it's a National Forest. There are enough gold seekers. We don't need people looking for the missing tribe."

"I agree. We don't want that. Long before this was a National Forest, long before the US was a nation, these people lived here. You know they'll be removed and sent to a reservation."

Cal threw his fingers through his hair. "You're probably right, but it's out of my control. It's something for the law to determine."

"The white man's law," Lil said.

"I'm just thinking off the top of my head. Maybe we contact an attorney who works in Native American law and see what they think." Cal said.

"We can do that. I have tomorrow afternoon off. What's your schedule look like?" Lil said.

"Start in the morning, but can see if I can get some coverage for the afternoon. I'm not sure we'll be able to see someone so quickly though," Cal said.

"I'll work on that. Let me know what time you can get off," Lil said, feeling a bit more optimistic.

"Depending on what they say, I may have to let the sheriff's department be aware of what is going on in the mountains."

"Let's just wait and see, Cal. See what they tell us," Lil said placing her hand on his. "Can I get you something to eat?"

"I should probably go," Cal said as he rose to his feet.

"Please stay. I want you to," Lil said as Cal wasn't sure what was best. "Cal, at least let me make you something. Pasta, something really simple."

"Sure, okay,"

Cal and Lil spent the next few hours looking at attorney firms in the Phoenix area that had experience in Native American law. They reviewed some sites and specific cases. It came down to three firms they felt comfortable with.

They moved back into the living room, taking notes on questions and scenarios they wanted to bring up. Cal leaned back on the couch and closed his eyes. He just needed to take a break for a few minutes. Within a few minutes, he was sound asleep. Lil went to the bedroom to get a blanket and placed it over him and turned off the light.

The next morning, Cal was out the door early. He headed home and then to the sheriff's office in Florence. He felt more rested, but emotionally he still struggled that no matter what he did, he was letting someone down. Spending the evening with Lil had helped a bit. He had feelings for her and he could sense she had them for him. He wasn't just being played.

* * *

The next morning, Jose was off to the Superstitions, hoping to have better luck than Cal and the other deputies. He needed some leads to work off of. The

Superstitions had taken many lives and many times leaving no clues.

It was a Friday, there was always an increase in hikers, and with that came an increase in rescues. He was at the Peralta trailhead as the sun was coming up over the Superstitions. The parking lot was already half full as the experienced hikers were out early.

For the next hour, Jose spoke with several hikers headed up the trail. No one had seen anything, but most said they would spread the news and have them contact Jose if anyone remembered seeing Jeff Albright. Jose was feeling frustrated. He was on a loan to help find an answer and there was nothing to go on.

"Jose, good morning," came a familiar voice.

Jose turned and saw Waylen. "Was there a call I didn't hear?"

"No, just doing some recreational hike myself," Waylen said as he adjusted his backpack.

"Well, good to know if someone gets in trouble. Want to take some of these fliers, see if anyone saw anything?"

"Sure thing. Any luck?" Waylen said as he took a handful of fliers.

"Nothing yet. I'm doing double duty in the sheriff's office. Trying to find something, anything. Something maybe out of the ordinary." Jose said.

"Well, maybe you should talk to Ranger Shanta. I guess she saw some lights the other night and came across some suspicious characters. Not sure what it was all about," Waylen said, all proud that he might have some information to help.

"I didn't know that. I'll get a hold of her. You never know, maybe it will lead to something."

"I'll hand out these fliers. If you need anything else, I'm always glad to help." Waylen said as he made his way up the trail.

Jose didn't have any better lead than Waylen's. He pulled out his cell phone and sent a text to Lil.

"You got a minute? I heard you came across a few suspicious people the other day. Call me when you can."

20

In the 1970s, several deaths occurred in the Superstition Mountains. In 1971, a 2nd lieutenant from Williams Air Force Base fatally crashed his T-38 Talon into the West side of the mountains. Additionally, a couple of hikers were killed, one by a boulder falling on him and the other falling over 60 feet. More concerning, there were also a half dozen people who were fatally shot in the Superstitions.[1]

* * *

Cal saw the text from Lil that Jose wanted to speak with her. He replied to her to stick to the story. Make it sound as generic as possible. He also let her know he could get off an hour early if she somehow could make an appointment with an attorney.

A call had come in that a few hikers looking for the Lost Dutchman Gold Mine had not been heard from in a few days. They began their journey in the Superstitions in Maricopa County, but Maricopa SAR requested that the Pinal SAR could cover trails on the border.

Waylen had radioed that he had gone up Peralta and was almost at Fremont Saddle and would head over to Weavers Needle. Jose was going to head towards Miners' Needle. He was hoping he might get lucky and get answers on Jeff Albright as well. A few other volunteers took different trails.

Cal replied he would go to First Water and head to the Massacre Grounds. Part of him was happy that he could take his mind off of the last few days and look for some lost hikers. Another part of him was thinking about all these people searching in the Superstitions. Someone was going to find this group of Native American villages. But he also knew with all the searches over the years, no one found them, or at least came forward on finding them.

Lil had the day off, so she was free to help in the search. She knew better than anyone where they would not want someone stumbling into this secret tribe. She radioed in she would head out to Iron Mountain.

Cal had a feeling he wouldn't find anything till he got to the Massacre Grounds and then from there, he would go off the trail. No one looked for the gold mine on the trails. He came across numerous hikers along the way, but no one saw anything unusual.

Once he made it to the Massacre Grounds, he headed due east. Cal took advantage of the high ground and took out his binoculars. He saw several longhorn sheep and a few hikers, but they didn't seem like the gold hunters he came across in the past. But he headed in their direction as they had seen something.

As he started his way toward the hikers, he heard helicopters to the north. The torn alliance of being a Search & Rescue deputy with the advantage of air surveillance and worrying about the mountain tribe's well-being was weighing heavily on him.

Lil was busy searching Iron Mountain and then planned to head to White Mountain. She hadn't come across any hikers. Lil had been split on her responsibilities as a Volunteer for the SAR along with her being a Ranger for the Tonto Forest. Keeping people from finding the hidden tribe in the Superstitions was a full-time job. She had set up an appointment in the late afternoon with a law firm, but it looked like that would not happen today.

Waylen and Jose, respectively, had encountered many hikers along their routes, but no one had seen anything unusual. The fliers on Jeff Albright came up empty as well.

It was the middle of the afternoon when it came over the radio that the helicopter had located the party in question. They were fine. They had turned their cell phones off, even though they probably would have no service, as they didn't want anyone to track their trek to where they believed the Lost Gold Mine was located.

As Lil headed back to her vehicle, she kept checking to see when she would be in cell service. She thought if she hustled she could make it to the attorney's office if Cal was back in time. She also knew Jose wanted to speak with her. The hike had given her time to think about how to answer questions he might have.

Sure enough, when Lil got into range, her phone came to life with several text messages. Cal could be in Apache Junction by 3:30 if she had found someone to speak with them. Jose had sent another text to see if she could meet this afternoon.

First thing she called the attorney's office and said they might be a little late, but no later than 4:30. She sent a text to Jose asking if they could meet in the morning. Lil saw the reply from the attorney's office confirming it was no issue with 4:30. She then sent a text to Cal that a firm agreed to meet with them in Scottsdale and she would meet Cal in Apache Junction.

Soon after that, they headed to Scottsdale. "Cal, how do we explain this?"

"Just lay it out and see what advice, if any, they have. If they tell me to inform the authorities, I will do that." Cal replied.

"I understand. You must do what you feel is right." Lil said as she hoped the lawyers would help her with his decision.

They entered the offices and were pleased to see it appeared to be an established and well-to-do firm. Their research the evening before had confirmed they had experience in the rights of indigenous people.

Lil and Cal were escorted into a small conference room. Lil walked around the room examining the artwork, which was much of that of the southwestern Native Americans that once roamed Arizona.

Cal took a seat facing the door as Lil sat next to him. After a few minutes, the door opened. A tall Native American woman entered and shook Cal and Lil's hands as they stood up. "Good afternoon, I'm Nita Summerhill. It's a pleasure to meet you," she said as she took a seat across from the two of them.

You mentioned you have an urgent matter and it has to do with Native American people. Is that correct?" she said as she opened a slim leather binder.

"That's correct," Cal answered.

She looked at Lil, "I can see you're Native American," then turned to Cal, "I'm guessing you might have some Native American blood in you,", not letting them answer. "So what is the situation we are looking at? Something to protect your rights? Is someone suing you?" She said with a fake smile.

"It's a bit more complicated than that," Cal said.

"We are looking to protect a large group of Native Americans, Salado's" Lil jumped in.

Lil got Nita Summerhill's attention, "Okay, let's make this official." As she pulled out a form from the binder. "This is just a basic contract. You sign this, make a payment, which confirms that we are representing you, and this way anything you tell me is a lawyer, client privileged."

"How much do you need?" Lil asked.

"The initial fee is $400," Ms. Summerhill replied.

"We just came from searching in the Superstitions looking for some hikers. We didn't bring a checkbook. Would a credit card do?" Cal said as he pulled out his wallet.

"Absolutely. Please review the form and fill in where appropriate. We can change it later if we need to." Ms. Summerhill said as she took Cal's credit card and left the room.

"Cal, you can't pay for this. It's a lot of money," Lil said, looking into his tired eyes.

"Don't worry about it. Let's see what she says." Cal said as he started filling out the form.

Within a few minutes, Ms. Summerhill returned with Cal's credit card and a receipt. Cal quickly filled in the remaining lines and handed the forms over to Lil. "Sign it as well. I put us both on here."

"Take your time and review it," Ms. Summerhill replied.

Lil went through the document quickly and then handed it back to her. "If we get a copy of this, we should be fine."

"Okay then, what is the situation?"

Cal leaned forward, then looked at Lil, "Bottom line, there are a few hundred people, a tribe if you will, of Native Americans living in the Superstition Mountains. For the most part, no one knows about them."

Nita Summerhill showed no emotions as she spoke, "How long have then been living there, Salado's you said?"

"Hundreds of years," Cal answered.

"Correct me if I'm wrong, but they are in a National Forest?" Nita said, knowing the answer as she began writing notes. "And where do the two of you come into play with this? Are you part of this group?"

Lil glanced at Cal then at Ms. Summerhill, "Yes and no, for me. I was born in the Superstitions, but I now reside in Apache Junction."

It hadn't occurred to Cal that Lil was born there as he listened to Lil and then turned to Ms. Summerhill. "I just found out about this in the last 48 hours. I'm coming to you," Cal paused, "We're coming to you because we're not sure what to do. I'm a deputy in the Search and Rescue in Pinal County. I feel it's my responsibility to let my superiors know about this."

"And why haven't you Mr. Ligai?"

"That's a question I'm struggling with," Cal answered.

"So what happened 48 hours ago that made you aware of this?"

"As you can appreciate, I'm involved in search and rescue with people every week in the Superstition Mountains. A few months ago a young boy was lost in the Superstitions. He was hiking with Ranger Shanta,"

Lil was a bit taken aback that he called her by her official title, "Yes, that's correct." Lil added.

Cal continued, "He came across one of their hidden villages. He didn't share it with anyone. A few months later, he took his sister there. Then the following day they came to me with what they found."

Ms. Summerhill continued to write notes, "And why did they come to you?"

"I'm not sure," Cal answered.

"Cal has a way with people. I'm sure they were comfortable with him and knew they could trust him." Lil added.

Cal told her about the young Salado Indian boy he had met with the kids and was spotted in the middle of the night at Freddy's window. He told them he spoke with the Apache Junction police and had a conversation with the kids' parents.

Ms. Summerhill closed her binder. "Well, I'm glad I stayed. This is, well, something significant. I plan on speaking with the partners about this. In the meantime, if possible, hold off telling anyone until I speak with you."

Cal was hoping to get something definitive today, "Any idea when you might be getting back to us?"

"Hopefully tomorrow. Ms. Shanta, we'll look into getting you some type of immunity since you have family there,"

Lil nodded, "Thank you. Cal's grandmother is up there as well."

"Okay, no one said anything about that," Ms. Summerhill continued. "I'm not sure if it will do any good in helping you keep your jobs, but maybe it will help keep you out of jail."

Lil turned to Cal, "I'm sorry I got you involved."

"At this point, I'm not sure any of this matters. I just want to get this taken care of," Cal answered.

The two left the office and headed for Lil's pickup. It was a quiet ride until they were a few minutes from Cal's truck.

"Cal, did you want to stay over tonight?"

"I have to drop the truck off at the office. I'll just stay in Florence," Cal replied.

"Okay, I forgot you had to take the truck back. I'm meeting Jose at the Sheriff's office tomorrow morning," Lil said hoping Cal would invite her to stay at his place.

"Just stick to the script. We need to buy a little more time."

Lil pulled up to Cal's truck. Cal turned to Lil as he got out of her pickup. "Let's hope we get some answers tomorrow."

* * *

The next morning, Lil drove out to Florence to meet Jose at the Pinal Sheriff's Office. Jose had his usual smile as Lil walked over to his desk.

"Good morning Lil, I appreciate you coming in."

"No problem. I'm up early anyhow."

"Well, I'm not sure if anyone told you, I'm kind of doing double duty, trying to help figure out what happened to Jeff Albright in the Superstitions."

"Yes, I heard about it. Did you find anything? I heard he died of a contusion to the head." Lil said.

"Yep. The coroner said it looks like a rock or could even be a fall. The funny thing is he didn't die where we found him. So three things could have happened. Somebody killed him with a rock and moved him. He died from a fall and then someone moved him for some reason, or third, but highly unlikely, an animal moved him. If that was the case, we would have seen evidence of that so, really only two scenarios that make sense."

"That sounds logical," Lil said, showing little emotion.

"I spoke with Waylen yesterday and he said the other night you came across a couple of shady characters."

"I'm not sure how shady. I saw some lights flickering and thought I would check it out. There was no record of anyone camping there overnight." Lil explained.

"So they were camping there?"

"They had a fire going, a couple of backpacks. I didn't see a tent. They seemed a bit surprised to see me."

"What time was this?"

"I'm not sure. It was very late. Probably after midnight." Lil said.

"Wow. That's late," Jose said as he wrote a few things.

"When I can't sleep, the mountains are cool and a good place to think. I'm not the only one. I guess Waylen was up there, too." Lil said with a bit of sarcasm.

"True. So Waylen says they walked you to your vehicle and you were talking to them about authorities going through the Superstitions."

"I guess I did, but they said little and I wanted them to think about that I wouldn't be the first person they would see if they were doing something illegal. I was a woman alone on a dark mountain with two men. Just a little psychology."

"Can you give me a description of them?"

"It was dark, but one about 6 feet, the other taller. Both had ball caps on and looked like brown hair. The taller one had blue eyes, brown for the other. I would say they both were 225 - 240 range."

Lil heard the doors open behind her and turned to see who it was. It was Cal who was headed to the desk to the right of Jose's.

Cal made eye contact with both of them. "Good morning, guys. Looks like everyone is starting their day off early."

"Good morning, Cal," Lil said as she turned back to Jose.

"Good morning brother," Jose said.

Jose continued to ask Lil additional questions as the office filled up as the morning shift was coming in. Cal was the first to see the Sheriff walking up to them.

"Good morning gentlemen, ma'am," the Sheriff said as he tilted his hat. "I thought of you boys in the Search and Rescue last night. Did you see in the redwoods in northern California there is someone claiming aliens have landed? Now he has gone missing. Let's not get involved with aliens or anything like that, no Bigfoot…" the Sheriff went on.

Lil couldn't help but interrupt "Or some secret tribe,"

"Right," the Sheriff laughed. "You come across any of that, you deal with it, don't get me involved."

Lil glanced at Cal as Jose broke out into a deep laugh. "We have all the gold hunters. We don't need aliens, Bigfoot, or anything, sir. Don't worry, we'll take care of it."

"When you get a chance, look at what's going on in California, it's just crazy."

The Sheriff walked away and Jose turned back to Lil, "Anything else?"

"That's about it. If I think of anything else, I'll let you know," Lil said as she stood up, shook Jose's hand, and nodded to Cal.

Jose leaned back in his chair. "Brother, I have nothing to go on except that Lil came across a few guys in the mountains the other night. She said they seemed a bit odd but didn't think much beyond that. I just wonder, is something going on up there, some smuggling? Maybe drugs or people?"

"A lot is going on up there. Usually, it's about gold." Cal said, hoping to defuse anything Lil shared with him.

"Yeah, you're probably right, but you never know."

"You aren't kidding," Cal said as he finished his last email before heading out.

It wasn't long before Cal received a phone call from Nita Summerhill. They were interested in representing Cal, Lil, and the entire hidden tribe. The practice's recommendation was to hold off on letting anyone know at this point. They would work with government agencies to see about protecting Cal and Lil and, more importantly, work on keeping this group of Native Americans in their homes.

21

Jacob Waltz died in 1891, and many believe that his lost gold mine is still out there. Many gold hunters, still today, search for the lost mine. Many have spent small fortunes looking for the mine and many have died searching.[1]

* * *

The only idea Jose had was maybe there was some smuggling of drugs in the Superstitions. Maybe Lil had come across these two people. Maybe this Jeff Albright ran into these men and his body was moved to destroy any evidence of wherever Jeff Albright had died.

He spoke to the Sheriff about his theory. The SAR had just been combing the mountains for the missing gold hunters and had not come across anything. So the question was, if there was a group of smugglers up there, how to find them or smoke them out?

It was decided to use Aurora 5, the new helicopter for night sweeps across the Superstitions. The sensitive heat sensor would pick up any movement in the night's darkness.   It was determined that sweeps of the Superstitions for three consecutive nights would uncover anything if there was in fact something to find. Because the theory was there could be drugs or human trafficking, they could work with State and Federal agencies to help pay for the costs.

The sweep of the mountains would start the next evening if the helicopter wasn't needed for anything else. They would continue the sweep for three nights. Jose and Austin were working on flight plans to maximize the coverage and utilize the heat sensors in Aurora 5.

"Let me give Cal a call, and see if he has any thoughts," Jose said to Austin.

"Yeah, sure thing,"

Jose called Cal's cell, hoping to catch him. "Hello" came Cal's voice.

"Brother, it's Jose and I'm here with Austin. We've got a green light for three nights of sweeps of the Superstitions with Aurora 5. We're hoping to find heat makers and therefore movement in the mountains. Any thoughts on any areas we should focus on, or just a general sweep." Jose said to Cal.

"How did you get that through? This is to help with finding out what happened with Jeff Albright." Cal questioned.

"Yeah. After speaking with Waylen and then Lil, maybe something is going on in the Supes. Maybe drug smuggling, maybe smuggling people. Both the state and Feds think it's worth a look and have funds to help with the budget."

"Overall, a general sweep is probably best, at least the first night. It's hard to say without seeing what you have in front of you," Cal replied.

"Are you close to the San Tan office? We'll be here for another hour," Austin chimed in.

"I am. I can be there in about 15 minutes. It will be interesting to see what you have planned," Cal said, as he truly wanted to see where they would be the next three nights.

"All right brother, we'll see you then," Jose said.

Cal not only wanted to know the flight path, but specifically what they would be looking for and what actions would be put in place if they were to find something. He sent a text to Lil, "Night sweeps with helicopters for the next three nights. They will use heat sensors to look for anything suspicious. We need to make sure nothing can be seen at night."

Cal was at the Sheriff's office in San Tan Valley within 15 minutes. Jose and Austin were in a small conference room in the back. They had a map of the Superstitions on the table and then the whiteboards around the room were filled up with specific locations.

"It looks like you guys have been busy," Cal said as he tried to soak in as much as he could.

"We have," Jose said with a big grin.

"At first we were looking at just the portions of the Superstitions that were in Pinal County, but with the State and Federal support we've expanded the scope," Austin said.

Cal looked down at the map and so two red stars were placed on it. "Looks like you've got where Jeff Albright's body was found. What is the second location?" Cal asked, knowing it was the site where Waylen had spotted Lil.

"Right, where the body was found and the second spot is where Lil came across those characters," Jose replied.

"That makes sense to start there. They are close, too?" Cal said, studying the map.

Austin pointed to the area. "Right, we'll plan to start our scan in that area. It could be the best chance to find something. From there, we plan on heading east. You can see where we're headed. The yellow highlights are the reach of the sensors."

"That's quite a large area it picks up. So it picks up heat. So hikers, campers animals you'll see it all?" Cal said, looking between the map and the whiteboards.

"Right. I think if we see anything that looks like two or more people, we'll zoom in and get a closer look. Take some photos and determine what we picked up. If anything of six or more people we might get close, right away. And if anyone takes off, we'll be in pursuit," Austin replied.

'Gentlemen, this looks really good. Anyway, can someone hide from detection of the infrared?" Cal inquired.

"That would have to be wrapped in aluminum foil or mylar from head to toe," Austin chuckled.

"Can I take some photos of the whiteboards and map? I'll go through it with a fine toothcomb tonight." Cal said, making a mental note of what Austin shared.

Jose gestured his arm to the whiteboards, "Go ahead. We'll appreciate your thoughts."

Cal pulled out his cell phone and started taking photos. Jose and Austin discussed the camera in the helicopter. Cal thought about the tribe's location and how to hide from the sensors.

"Cal, if you have any thoughts, shoot me an email. I'm going home for a bit to try to get some sleep. It's going to be a long night,"

"It sure will be. I'll send both of you my thoughts and any suggestions." Cal said as he made his way to the door. Next stop to Lil's, examining the map and routes of the next three evenings.

Cal was thinking about the aluminum foil comment that Austin made. Of course, they couldn't produce clothes made of aluminum foil or mylar, but there might be a way to keep Aurora 5 from finding the hidden tribe. They, of course, had mylar blankets they used for lost hikers who needed to be warmed up. How could they replicate that on a large scale? The moon would also be out, so any aluminum or mylar would stand out to the normal eye.

Then it hit him. Buy as many mylar foil sheets from every home improvement store they could find and spray one side with flat black paint.

When he got to Lil's, he explained to her his thoughts. "I don't know the setups of all the villages. Would hanging large canopies help? Canopies to cover tunnel entrances where heat might escape?" Cal asked.

"That could work. Of course, a good portion of the villages are already out of view but that would come in handy in the cliff dwelling and vent holes." Lil replied.

"We'll need to purchase every can of black spray paint we can find. Are there people that can start on that? Then get them out to the villages?" Cal said as he paced in the kitchen.

Lil picked up her cell and started texting, "Working on it now."

"Okay, great, let's look at these flight plans. Figure out what we need to do."

The two went over each plan and worked in approximate estimated times of the path for the next few hours. They looked at key locations and what angle the helicopter would come at. Lil was making notes for the number of foil sheets she thought they would each need.

When they felt they had a good handle on what they needed to do, Lil turned to Cal, "I think I'm going to go up there tonight to each village."

"That sounds like a good plan,"

"The rolls of foil are being dropped off at a warehouse we have access to in Apache Junction. I'll send you the address. Maybe you could help with spraying them black," Lil suggested.

"Perfect," Cal said as they both headed out the door.

As Lil stepped into her vehicle, she turned to Cal. "Thank you," she paused, "Be careful."

* * *

That evening, Lil went to the Great House where she took Cal to. She spoke in great detail with the elders there, on the helicopter with infrared night vision. She explained that Cal and a group are painting foil tarps.

"We need to cover the cliff dwellings and cover any vents where heat might escape. All fires must be extinguished for the next few days," Lil explained.

The elders sat and listened and finally, the oldest replied, "So Calian is helping us," and the others nodded in agreement.

"Yes. He also spoke with a law practice to see what legal things could be done to keep anyone from making us leave."

"So others now know of us?" one elder asked.

"Yes. But by law, they can't divulge any information to anyone." Lil replied.

"White man laws. We must be cautious."

"The attorneys are Native Americans. I feel there is no reason for concern at this time."

"Let's hope you're correct. Tomorrow morning, we will survey the area and determine the placement of these tarps."

* * *

Cal, Linda Sharper, Michael Kowalski, and others were spraying foil tarps and creating stacks of tarps for the villages of the Superstitions.

Linda Sharper looked at the clock on the wall, just after 2 AM, and walked over to Cal. "I think those are the last two tarps. We'll take them all up to the villages in the morning. Anything else we need, any directions?"

"Just make sure the tarps overlap if needed. We don't want any seams. Make sure they all understand there are to be no fires for the next few days. Make sure everyone understands anyone out in the open will be seen with their cameras."

"Cal, thank you for helping all of us. These people deserve to remain in their homes."

"I'll do what I can. First things first. Let's get through the next few nights. I still have a lot of questions. I'm still trying to figure out how you and Michael Kowalski, go into the Superstitions. You were called in missing in the Superstitions and you decide to stay. You left loved ones behind." Cal said.

"Life is always changing. Our roles change. We look for where we can do the most good for others. If you spend more time with us, you will find your answers."

* * *

Early that morning, the foil tarps were all delivered to the villages. Lil made her way to the other three villages to reinforce what they needed to do over the next three nights.

The timing of the tarps would need to be done quickly as the sun set and not be visible to any hikers that may walk nearby.

Cal had gotten a few hours of sleep before reporting to the sheriff's office in Florence. He was hoping for a quiet day. Jose had left him an email that he would be in the helicopter the next few evenings and thanked him for reviewing the routes.

The night shift for SAR was wrapping up a rescue on Flatiron in the Superstitions. Cal headed out as it gave him an excuse to be in the Superstitions. Lil had left him a cryptic text that she had been at all the villages and the tarps were being delivered and everything would be set for this evening.

By the time Cal got to Dutchman State Park, the rescue was all wrapped up. He stayed in the Supes for a little while, but things were quiet, so he headed to the sheriff's station in San Tan Valley. Cal finished some reports that he had not completed, as his mind was elsewhere the last few days. When Cal's shift was over, he intended to get a few hours of sleep and be up and ready to listen to the radio chatter from the helicopter as it flew over the Superstitions.

He sent a text to Lil that she might want to join him at his place to hear it as well. She had first replied that she thought it might be best to be in the Supes for the next three nights. Cal shared he thought she might be more valuable in determining what they were looking at on infrared night vision.

Cal was up by 7 PM and listening to the radio. He laid out a large map of the Superstitions on his kitchen table and placed a coin to where he thought the helicopter was, based on the flight path and the conversations on the radio. Cal knew they would first be concentrating on the area where they found Jeff Albright's body. The closest village was far enough away that they shouldn't be focusing in that direction.

Lil arrived shortly after 9 PM and Cal updated her on the helicopter's activity. The two weren't sure how effective the tarps would be, but they felt comfortable that the first village the helicopter was going to go over directly was smaller than the others and had less direct vision of the open sky.

For the most part, the first few hours were generic. They came across numerous wildlife including longhorn sheep, bobcats, javelinas, and coyotes. They came across a few campers, but nothing out of the ordinary. Cal could hear them record the location of the campers and would be checked out the next day.

From Cal and Lil's best guess, they would soon fly over the smallest village within the next fifteen minutes. The two of them hung on to every word they heard.

"Nothing showing up… pretty dark down there, not even a coyote." came Jose's voice on the radio.

"Over there, we're picking something up. Turn to the north," came another voice.

There was what felt like a long silence to Cal and Lil until they heard Austin's voice. "I don't see anything. I'll go back to our flight plan."

Lil turned to Cal, "I wonder if it was the village they saw or something else?"

"Not sure. We'll have to let them know in the village if we find out if they saw something light up, even for a second. Make sure everything is secure." Cal replied.

They continued to listen the entire evening taking shifts, although they would wake each other when they felt the helicopter was getting close to one of the villages. No red flags were raised in the second village, which made Cal feel relieved.

The Great House was a bit of a scare. The infrared picked up some faint heat, but the area was so large that they dismissed it as a mountain formation that was still warm from the full day of the desert sun. The last village went unnoticed.

Cal turned to Lil. "I need to get some sleep before I head to work. You're free to crash here."

Lil smiled, "Thank you. I think I will. Not working the morning, but I think I'll be busy when I'm done going to the two villages."

"Take my bed. I'll crash on the couch." Cal said as he pulled out an extra pillow from the closet.

"Sure," Lil replied as she headed for the bedroom.

Lil was exhausted but couldn't fall asleep knowing Cal was on his couch, so close. She got out of bed and went into the living room where Cal was asleep. He looked so peaceful. She lay next to him and scooted her body along his. Still half asleep, Cal put his arm around Lil and she quickly fell asleep.

*   *   *

The next morning, Cal and Lil decided they would head to the Great House, which was close to where she would be stationed in the Tonto Forest. Cal would get to the first village sometime during the day where Jose's team thought they had seen something for a minute.

When Cal got to the sheriff's office, he was surprised to still see Jose and his team there. They were reviewing places they saw hikers or something out of the ordinary.

They had a list of locations on the whiteboard and a map on the conference room table. Cal laughed to himself as it looked like his kitchen table last night. He saw a list of names, including his on the whiteboard, with a few locations.

"Brother, I've already cleared it. If nothing comes up, can you check out these locations?" Jose said as he patted Cal on the back.

"Absolutely," Cal said as he looked at the locations, then the map. Then he saw that the location of the first and third villages was on the map. They were being checked by Deputy Gillen.

"Hey, looking at this map, why don't I take the third list? I'll switch with Gillen," Cal said, pointing to the whiteboard.

"Really? I'm trying to make it easy on you, giving you some easier locations."

"Thanks, but few of us know these mountains as well as you and I do. I can probably navigate that list with more ease than anyone else."

"If that's what you want," Jose said, making some changes on the whiteboard.

Cal jotted down the notes on all the locations he was to check and then headed out the door. Cal sent a text to Lil that he was going to the two villages, one that Lil planned on hiking out to. There was no need for her to go up there. If it remained quiet, he could take care of any issues.

Sure enough, when Cal got to the first village, they said they had noticed the tarps weren't overlapping as the helicopter was approaching. They quickly fixed it before the helicopter made its second pass. Cal went on to the next two locations on the list where they had seen hikers. The first one had traces of a small fire but they had already moved on. The next location, a tent, was still there as a young couple was making lunch.

The radio remained quiet, as Cal was hoping. He headed to the Great House, which had left a slight heat mark. He knew there would be several large tarps covering the large cliff structures. They would either need additional ones or somehow reduce any heat from the structure. He also knew if Deputy Gillen or anyone else came to check out the area, it would be all over. A remedy was needed before tonight.

When Cal arrived at the Great House, he met with the elders and explained the situation. They showed him how the tarps hung and there were no gaps. Cal had seen some cooking in one section and told them they had to eliminate all fires till this was all over. It wasn't just the evening. The only solution they came up with was to get additional tarps and double up and when they heard the helicopters approaching, have as many people as possible enter the caves and lava tubes, moving away from the tarps.

Cal would have felt better if there was something that stood out instead of guessing what the issue was. The tribe was resistant to any type of radio to communicate. They felt it was the white man's witchcraft, so Cal would contact Lil when he got into cell phone service. Cal radioed into the sheriff's office that all the areas he had checked showed up as clear, nothing but a few hikers camping.

By late afternoon, Lil was on her way to the Great House with additional tarps. Cal figured tonight was going to be like last night. He stopped at the office to see if there were any changes from the original flight plans. Jose wasn't in, but looking at the whiteboards, it appeared they were keeping the same path. Anything that showed heat last night would get an additional pass-over.

Cal headed home. He was exhausted, but he knew Lil was just as tired and she was headed back to the Great House with more tarps. Cal didn't expect her to join him tonight to listen to the radio. He sat on the couch and figured he would close his eyes for a few minutes.

22

The shared beauty of the Superstitions draws thousands of people to these mysterious mountains. Over the last fifty years, approximately fifty people have died in the mountains and the numbers increase yearly. Many succumbed to the harsh elements. Others became lost and disoriented, only to have their remains found years later.

* * *

Cal was woken by a voice on the radio on a different channel. "Wind. Wind". Cal looked outside. It was almost dark already. He must have slept for some time.

"Wind. Wind." came the radio.

Cal walked to the window. The trees and bushes were violently thrashing in the wind.

"Wind, wind," came the voice on the radio.

It sounded like Lil. "Sure is windy," Cal responded in a mono-tone voice as he wasn't sure who might monitor the channel.

"My father's place lost four shingles. " Lil said.

"Does he have any replacements?" Cal asked.

"Not with him. He has some in his unit. Was hoping his friend Mr. White would get them for him." Lil replied.

Mr. White, Cal rolled his eyes. He knew he was Mr. White. "I'm sure Mr. White will get them before any rain," Cal responded.

Cal was out the door within minutes, headed to the warehouse where they had additional painted tarps. Cal could feel his truck sway in the wind. Was it too windy for Aurora 5 to go up tonight? He hadn't heard anything on the radio yet. He couldn't take a chance. Either way, he had to bring as many tarps up as possible.

Cal pulled into the parking lot of the warehouse and went to the main entrance to find the door locked. He went around the building to look for another entrance. The back door was locked as well. He knew time wasn't on their side.

He saw a window in the back was opened but it was a good five to six feet from the ground. Cal quickly pulled his truck under the window and hoisted himself through. Luckily, there were tables under the window on the inside.

Cal pointed the flashlight in the direction where he remembered the tarps were. He saw a small stack and headed for it. When he approached, he was concerned, as he only counted three remaining. He gathered the three and headed out the back door.

As he got in the car, he heard Austin and Jose on the radio. They were going to get a late start because of the high winds, but the winds were projected to abruptly stop within an hour. It gave Cal a little more time, but he only had three tarps.

He turned his channel and slowly spoke. "Three shingles, three shingles."

There was no reply and as he drove, he repeated the message. A few minutes later, he heard a reply, "Father needs four."

"Sounds like one short. Did your father check the area for a shingle?" Cal answered.

"Yes, he is looking now, but no luck so far." Came Lil's voice.

"Hopefully, he'll find one. It looks like the rain might be an hour later than expected," Cal replied.

"Good to know we have time. I wonder if Mr. White can stop at another location to retrieve a shingle." Lil said.

Another location. Did he think he had time to go to a store and spray paint it and then get it to the Great House? He did the math in his head and wasn't sure he could get there in time.

"Another location? Purchase more shingles?" Cal replied.

"No, I think he wants them before the rain. Maybe one of the other houses constructed at the same time has a shingle to spare."

"They might need theirs, but I'll check it out," Cal responded, figuring he would go to the one village that was closest to the Great House and see if they had one they could spare.

Cal continued to monitor Aurora 5 as it was in the air now headed to the Superstitions. In another twenty minutes, Cal was on foot, headed to the village. He did the math in his head and projection of the Aurora 5. If he was correct, he would arrive at the first village just before Aurora 5 flew over.

He continued to calculate his time of arrival. If anything, it kept him motivated to get there quickly. He didn't want to get caught out in the open when the helicopter flew over. In the darkness, Cal wasn't sure how far he had to go, but he thought he was close. Then he heard it coming from behind him, Aurora 5. He would not make it to the village in time. Aurora 5 was moving faster than he projected.

There was nowhere to find coverage, so pulled out one tarp as Aurora 5 was gaining on him. He threw the tarp over himself. Did he get undercover quickly enough? He wasn't sure. He could hear the helicopter for what seemed like an eternity until finally the noise of its engines slowly faded away.

If the helicopter continued at that pace, he wasn't sure he could get to the Great House in time to get the tarps in place. He monitored the helicopter on the radio. They weren't seeing much besides wildlife. When Cal arrived at the village, he told them that the Great

House needed one of their tarps. They quickly gathered one and Cal was off the Great House.

In the darkness, Cal felt he was moving too slowly. He couldn't make it in time. Cal could see the Aurora 5 periodically making passes to the south of his location, each time getting closer to the Great House. He came across a fork in the canyon and he knew he was about twenty minutes away.

Again he could hear Aurora 5 in the distance. It was going to be very close. Cal could see the helicopter turn in the distance and head his way. He wasn't going to make it. He pulled out his radio and turned the channel.

"Five minutes out with four shingles. I think the rain will be there at the same time. Won't have time to put shingles up." Cal said.

"Understood." came Lil's voice.

Cal ran as he saw the helicopter light getting closer and closer. After tonight, the lost tribe of Salado would be known. The lights seemed to be almost over the Great House when the helicopter made an abrupt turn to the south.

The canyon wall blocked Cal's view to the south. Three large flares had shot up. As the helicopter saw them, they turned to see what was happening. Cal continued to keep moving forward. Within a few minutes, Lil and a group of people took the tarps from Cal and quickly set them up, knowing the helicopter would be back.

"Cal, are you all right?" Lil asked, helping him to an interior room.

"Yes. I'm not sure why the helicopter turned, but I'm not going to complain." Cal said as he drank some water.

"Let's just say we had some friends help with a distraction. They'll get those tarps up quickly. We actually found one of them once the winds died down. We'll double up where we can." Lil said, squeezing Cal's hand.

The tarps were all in place when they heard the engines of Aurora 5 continue on their original path. The helicopter continued and could be heard later in the evening to the north, but apparently, nothing of the Great House showed up.

Cal and Lil both slept there that evening. They felt peaceful and in touch with the mountain. The following morning, they headed home and to their respective jobs. Cal had the following afternoon off and was hoping to catch up on sleep, but with everything going on, that was far from a guarantee.

Jose had left two locations to check out that morning. None were of the villages. Additional deputies were sent to the third location, where there was some type of flares or fire that evening. Lil had sent a text to Cal that the two tarps that had been blown away were recovered and one was being sent to the village where Cal had borrowed one. That evening Cal and Lil listened over the radio on the final evening of the flyover of the Superstitions. It was an uneventful evening and Cal and Lil were more than happy about this.

The next morning, Lil left and Cal got some additional sleep. When he finally woke, he saw he had missed a message from Nita Summerhill. He quickly made a cup of coffee and called her office.

After being put on hold for five minutes, Nita picked up.

"Cal, thank you for getting back to me. I have what I feel is some good news. My office has been on the phone quite a bit the last few days."

"I'm ready for some good news. It's been a long few days," Cal replied.

"Bottom line, the US Department of the Interior Indian Affairs is very interested in what is happening here. First, if the tribe in the Superstitions told you they are descendants and see themselves as the Salado tribe. The United States does not currently have a treaty with them. They are actually in the middle of trying to pass a law in Congress. They would like to add something to this law that would keep any indigenous people from being removed from their current homes. That would include the Salado tribe."

"Damn, that would be wonderful. It's been weighing on me that I've been keeping this from my supervisors." Cal said.

"I'm afraid that's where it gets a little sticky. Ideally, this law could be passed in six months, but it could take a few years. In the meantime, we don't want anyone to find out about the Salado tribe in the Superstitions. We don't want to take a chance that Homeland or someone will try to remove them." Nita explained.

"That's putting a lot of pressure on me, and well, Lil as well."

"Everyone can appreciate that. We will have amnesty and full pardons from the US Government for you and Ms. Shanta. But we need you to help us continue to keep them hidden, from the public as well as local and state agencies."

"If Lil and I will have full amnesty and pardons, why can't we at least bring the Pinal Sheriff's Department up to speed on this?" Cal replied, as his frustration could be heard by Nita.

"It's not that simple. I'll see what we can do, but the more people who know about this, the greater the risk. They may not feel the same way you and Ms. Shanta feel. Also, since you and Ms. Shanta are at least partially Native American, it gives us more weight to give you full pardons." Nita explained.

"I guess I understand, but I sure hope this is closer to six months than two years."

"We all do. And remember, the fewer people who know, probably the less there is to pardon. We have another sticky point, the two kids you mentioned. How old are they and is the secret safe with them?" Nita asked.

"I'll find out their ages but both minors, teenagers. I think they can be trusted." Cal told her.

"I'm counting on you to monitor the situation with them. Finally, I'll need you and Ms. Shanta to come in for a DNA test to prove your heritage. Other than that, please be patient."

"Thank you. I'll do whatever is needed," Cal said as the conversation ended.

Although it was not exactly what Cal wanted to hear, he felt at peace for the first time in days. He sent a text to Lil that he spoke with Nita Summerhill and all was good and if she wanted to have dinner. He then sent a text to Jose to see how the final evening with Aurora 5 went. Within minutes, Cal's cell phone rang.

"Brother! Thank you for all your help over the last few days. I guess we came up empty. The case will be closed. The good thing is I'm back on Search and Rescue full time," Jose said.

"Welcome back. A change of pace for you the last week. Now, back to reality." Cal said, relieved that they came up empty. He didn't need eyes in the Superstitions looking for any hidden secrets.

"Good to be back. Looks like our shift starts in the afternoon tomorrow. We'll catch up then. I have some interesting things to share."

"Yep, see you then," Cal replied.

That evening, Cal went to pick up Lil for dinner. He was thinking about a new restaurant in town. He heard it was a little fancy, but figured they deserved it. Lil opened the door, her hair in a ponytail, and a T-shirt and cut-off shorts. Cal looked at her, thinking the new restaurant was out.

"Cal, can we eat in? I'm making some of your favorites, Apache Stew and fried bread." Lil said with a big grin.

Cal stepped inside, closed the door and took Lil by the arm, and pulled her in. "You had me when you opened the door," Cal said and kissed her.

As the two remained embraced, Lil looked up at Cal, "Cal, I have fallen in love with you. I hope you know that?"

"I do," Cal said, not letting her go.

Eventually, the two ate their dinner and Cal told her about the conversion with Nita Summerhill and that Jose and his team came up empty on any leads. They found nothing more unusual than normal in the mountains. After they cleaned up after dinner, they made their way to the back patio and sat in a recliner that looked out at the Superstition Mountains.

A bright half-moon made the Superstitions look even more mysterious than normal.

"It really is an incredible, beautiful place," Cal said as he sipped his drink.

"Since man set his foot on these mountains, they have always been filled with magic and mystery," Lil replied.

"Yeah. I understand why the Salado don't want to leave. Why they fought for hundreds of years to keep their home?" Cal said, keeping his eyes on the mountain.

"And you, Mr. Ligai, whether you want to believe it, are helping the Salado tribe. In their mind you are the White Warrior," she said as she clutched his hand.

"I'm thinking it's a stretch. I will help them, we will help them. Hopefully, over the next six months, maybe a year, the Salado tribe will be recognized and will remain in the Superstitions." Cal said, turning to Lil.

"One less secret, Cal."

"Yes, but I think there will always be hidden secrets in the Superstitions."

* * *

In the months to follow Cal and Lil continued to help keep the Salado tribe unnoticed by the outside world. As Calian Ligai continued this endeavor more secrets from the past were uncovered while more were made.